RAWHIDERS OF THE BRASADA

Rawhiders of the Brasada

L. L. Foreman

WHEELER
CHIVERS

This Large Print edition is published by Wheeler Publishing, Waterville, Maine, USA, and by BBC Audiobooks Ltd, Bath, England.

Wheeler Publishing is an imprint of Thomson Gale, a part of The Thomson Corporation.

Wheeler is a trademark and used herein under license.

The text of this Large Print edition is unabridged.

Other aspects of the book may vary from the original edition.

Set in 16 pt. Plantin.

LIBRARY OF CONGRESS CATALOGING-IN-PUBLICATION DATA

Foreman, L. L. (Leonard London), 1901–
   Rawhiders of the Brasada / by L. L. Foreman.
     p. cm. — (Wheeler Publishing large print Western)
   ISBN 1-59722-391-3 (pbk. : alk. paper) 1. Large type books. I. Title.
  PS3511.O427R39 2006
  813'.54—dc22

2006029078

BRITISH LIBRARY CATALOGUING-IN-PUBLICATION DATA AVAILABLE

Published in 2006 in the U.S. by arrangement with
Golden West Literary Agency.

Published in 2007 in the U.K. by arrangement with Golden West Literary Agency.

U.S. Softcover: ISBN 13: 978-1-59722-391-1; ISBN 10: 1-59722-391-3
U.K. Hardcover: 978 1 405 63996 5 (Chivers Large Print)
U.K. Softcover: 978 1 405 63997 2 (Camden Large Print)

Printed in the United States of America on permanent paper
10 9 8 7 6 5 4 3 2 1

Rawhiders of the Brasada

I

Among the changes that Jim Madigan had observed in recent years was the attitude of cattlemen toward their cattle. Gone were the free and easy days when a hungry man might shoot and butcher a yearling, giving the owner its hide if he asked for it, no hard feelings. In the thriving beef market a cow these days was money on the hoof, good money, and cattlemen everywhere took a harsh view of the casual old custom.

Madigan tried to tell Jay Trubbidge that they couldn't expect Texas cattlemen to be any different in that respect, but Jay would have none of it. Jay was a rawhider, one of the special breed of wagon-wanderers whose customs and habits belonged to a bygone age, and he had inherited their intolerance of change.

"You've been out of Texas three or four years," Madigan reminded him.

Jay laughed. "What diff'ence that make?

It's a real man's country — always was, always will be! Real folks here!"

So here they were, standing off four armed and earnestly determined Texas cowpunchers.

The fresh cowhide still gave off a faint steam in the hot afternoon sun, but the exposed surfaces of the partly butchered carcass were taking on a dry glaze, speckled by a swarm of flies. Ought to cover it under a tarp pretty soon, Madigan thought, to keep it from spoiling. He reached over to brush away the flies, and promptly a bullet screamed inches above his fire-spotted wreck of a hat. He huddled down flat again and looked to see if Jay was all right.

Jay fired a return shot from his repeating rifle and called softly, "They're gettin' closer, Jim!" His blue eyes blazed. He stroked his rifle lovingly. "Betcha I can pick 'em off 'fore they reach them rocks!"

Madigan took note that his color was dangerously high and that he spoke jerkily, short of breath. "Take it easy," he told him. What he meant was: *Don't work yourself up into another fit!*

The four cowpunchers had yanked around when Madigan had waved them off, and had put their horses over the ridge. It had seemed they'd gone their way, prudently

taking the plain hint, but they had come
dodging back afoot, shooting, making a serious affair of it.

"Let's blow," Madigan said.

Jay, sighting his rifle, lowered it, sighing.
"Guess we better. I could bust 'em, though,
give you my word."

"Sure. But why?" Madigan eased down
the cocked hammer of his old carbine. "It's
most likely their steer we beefed."

"What o' that? How many times I gotta
tell you folks here don't ever mind a man
beefin' a cow for grub? This is Texas. It ain't
your goddam yankeeland where they charge
a man money to graze his horse!"

That was a Judas dig. Jay had once run
afoul of a new settler somewhere north who
wanted half a dollar for grass and a dime
for water. It stuck in his memory, clouding
his opinion of a dozen states and territories.

"Those four jiggers mind, and I'm not
surprised," Madigan said. "You keep forgetting I once lived down here."

"Yeah, but you ain't no Texan."

"No. I'm American."

Jay broke out a wry grin, sorry as usual
for flashing his temper at Madigan, who
rarely showed anger. He liked Jim Madigan,
the northerner, the damyankee. They had
drifted and worked together for two years,

9

ever since they'd met in a Wyoming-bound trail crew. In those two years they had ridden far: away up to Canada, down through the Southwest, and aslant into Texas — "Real man's country, Jim, b'lieve me!"

Madigan didn't believe in Texas or in any other claimed heaven on earth. He had ridden down to it with Jay because of some recollections, because he had been at loose ends with nothing better to do, and because he'd felt that Jay ought to have somebody with him in case he threw another fit.

Jay insisted that his fits were nothing more than attacks of indigestion, acquired from eating half-cooked yankee grub. He wanted to find his own folks and treat his abused stomach to real food. To trace their shifting whereabouts, he and Madigan had dropped in on rawhider camps, making inquiries.

The four cowpunchers were apparently holding a council of war before making their next move. "Okay, let's git," Jay said. "You first."

"No — you. I'll cover." Madigan saw him press a hand to his chest, breathing fast and hard. "Don't rush it!"

"Don't you git hurt. I'd have hell packin' you out o' here. You're a heavy big tramp, y'know."

"I am," Madigan agreed. He was large,

loosely built, weighing close to two hundred pounds when fed regularly. "I'm a big tramp."

"Funny thing, you don't ever look it. Can't even smell you."

"That's only because I wash and shave, when there's any water," Madigan said. Time was running short, but he wanted Jay to cool off and get a better hold on himself. He put on Jay's Texas drawl, exaggerating it, straight-faced. "Ah hev no bugs on me, ma'am, to mah best knowledge!" It was a reference to a certain Denver Lulu who, after fastidiously demanding from Jay his vows of personal purity, had given him a plague of assorted vermin.

"You son!" Jay grinned, scratching himself reminiscently, the tight look on his face loosening. "Ready? Here we go!"

They went, Jay first, then Madigan, running down into what Jay called a *potrero,* a sunken swale below sight of the four cowpunchers. There they legged aboard their horses and raced out, bent over and spurring. A flurry of shots cracked after them, snap fire at long range, doing no harm.

Later, making sure they weren't pursued, they reined down to a walk and swapped complaints and a trifle of philosophy.

"It ain't right, way they jumped us!" Jay

said. "Dammit, Jim, it ain't decent!"

He was embarrassed as well as indignant. Having, as he thought, talked Madigan into coming to Texas with him, he took the stand that he was host, Madigan his guest. He had talked glowingly of Texas as the finest, friendliest place on earth, a country where the stranger was welcome to help himself freely to practically anything except the women. The welfare of their womenfolk, he said, stood as a sacred trust to all Texas men.

Time and distance lent enchantment, Madigan guessed. He had observed on lonely Texas ranches many a toilworn woman whose welfare, he thought, could be considerably improved without reaching way up loftily to any sacred trust. He didn't mention it.

"You've been long gone, Jay," he said. "Times change."

"Not here!" Jay disagreed. "Not that-away!"

Local pride was the damnedest thing, Madigan mused. He had seen changes come to many places, some good, some bad. Because he belonged nowhere, he was not blind to them. He said, reasoning out loud, "We're living off the country. It's not like we've got something to give back for what we take — not like we own any cattle. I've never been anywhere they didn't mistrust the likes of us. And they're right! That includes Texas."

"You ain't a Texan," Jay countered. It threatened to become his favorite rejoiner. To be born in Texas endowed some kind of mystical privilege, a superiority beyond the understanding of the less fortunate. He fell silent a moment to track out his own line of reasoning. "I got to tell you, Jim — you did wrong when you waved off them four jiggers. They musta figgered us for a coupla rustlers. It made us look like it, see?"

"I see. I don't blame 'em." Madigan didn't crack a smile. Jay had beefed somebody's steer without leave, but it was the waved hat that did the damage. Oh, well. . . .

Establishing that satisfying conclusion, Jay perked up and spoke brightly of the green hill-country ahead where, at last report, his folks had been camped. Deer and wild turkey in the woods for the taking. Good fishing. Horses and cattle just naturally couldn't help prospering on the fine grazing.

"I've seen it," Madigan mentioned absently, his mind tugging at the past. "Lived up the valley from Sanburn, with my three brothers. Raised cattle." Raised hell, too, said memory.

"Well, I be dogged!" exclaimed Jay. "You

did? Right close near the Big Bend country, huh?" The reticence of the big, quiet man constantly puzzled him. After two years he knew next to nothing of Madigan's past — whereas he, talkative by nature, had told the story of his life several times over. "I didn't know you had any brothers."

"Haven't now. They died." Died violent deaths, all three. The Mad Madigans.

Since then he had pursued too many green hills. Far away, the hills showed green and promising, soft like a woman in dim light, heartening like a vision of home long lost. You strained to reach them, and found catclaw and mesquite and needle grass, dry creeks, dried-out people, gnarled and prickly. The green hills far away were bogus, the soft woman turned hard, the vision of home was a mirage. With tolerantly cynical humor he pushed his search, laughing at himself.

His personal cleanliness he had excused to Jay, once, when Jay had fidgeted impatiently by a mountain stream while Madigan had bathed himself and scrubbed his clothes: "A man's got to believe in something, if it's only soap. . . ."

Jay believed in Texas, in himself, and in the girl he said was waiting to marry him. He wasn't sold on dipping into every patch

14

of water along the route. But, liking Madigan, respecting him without quite knowing why, he overlooked the idiosyncrasy. Yankees were all kinda odd, and Madigan was one of the oddest.

Inquisitive, Jay wanted to dip further into Madigan's ranching days. Madigan turned it off by asking him about his girl. "Three years is a long time to wait. How old was she when you left?"

"I dunno. Fifteen, mebbe sixteen." Jay wasn't too sure of his own age. "My Arabella's waitin' for me, don't you worry!"

Madigan wagged his head, smiling. "Every rawhider camp we've called at, seems to me there's always an Arabella and a John Wesley. And those old Bible names! Luke, Daniel, Zeke, Ruth, Patience —"

"Us rawhiders are might religious," Jay agreed seriously. He had never seen the inside of a church, as far as Madigan knew, but he tipped his hat whenever he passed one, no matter what the denomination.

They made a dry and hungry camp that night, and were on their way before sunup. Trying to cheer things up on growling stomachs and cotton palates, Jay rattled off about the green hills ahead. Madigan stayed silent, remembering the green hills that had beckoned him back north a thousand miles.

15

They hadn't been bogus, no, those hills of his homeland, but they had become alien to him. He had found nothing up there that was for him, nothing to satisfy his restless searching.

Deliberately, he thought now of his brothers. He had been the youngest. After their parents had died, they'd sold out and moved down to Texas. A bad move. Back home they had gained a reputation for wildness, which had been one of the reasons for leaving. In Texas they had found broader scope, no parental restraint.

They'd bought a brand, thrown up a shack, and taken to hunting outlaw cattle in the Brasada. The Mavericking Madigans, darkly suspected of rustling. Trouble. They hadn't been able to ride into Sanburn and out again without getting into fights. The Mad Madigans, defying all the settled ranchers of the valley. Going off to hire out their guns wherever fighting pay was offered.

"Need the money to build up our spread, don't we?"

Spending every dollar, riding home broke, laughing over it.

It couldn't have gone on. The first death had sobered them only for a summer, the second for less than that. But when the last

16

of his three brothers had died, Jim Madigan had sold the spread and taken his northward trek alone.

He dated that year as the year when he became a quiet kind of man, seeking only what a Mexican would call perhaps his *querencia* — his haven, his place of the heart. It struck him as ironic that he had come full circle and returned to Texas.

II

Yet the hills ahead did stay green in the early morning sunshine. They grew greener on the approach. No familiar and disillusioning clumps of mesquite, catclaw; no needle grass.

"By jing, they *are* green!" Madigan muttered.

"Why, sure!" Jay said, with the air of having arranged it. I done tol' you, didn't I?"

"You did. I don't recall moseying round this particular piece of country before." Madigan watched a creek threading the bottom of a narrow draw. "Clear water. Must be springs here."

"Soldier Springs, yeah." Jay knew every spring and creek from San Antonio to El Paso, and every cattle brand. His eyes

17

shone. The homecoming look.

The live oaks and cottonwoods here were all in full leaf, and the grass grew that fresh and tender its green blended into the sky like water, like the sea at its horizon. Black-eyed susan and lavender verbena and bluebonnet splashed every fold of the hills with glorious colors. Even the everpresent prickly pear, hilarious clown of the cactus kingdom, shone a soft green, the thorns not yet hardened brown, the waxy blossoms flaring yellow around the edges of the ludicrous great fleshy leaves.

" 'Bout this time," Jay murmured knowledgeably, "my folks oughta be up Hunter Creek." He turned his expectant face to Madigan and said, "My folks are rawhiders from way back. *Wa-aay* back! You ain't seen rawhiders till you seen my folks!"

Madigan had seen rawhiders, not only while with Jay, but when he and his brothers had ranched on the edge of the Big Bend. The rawhider outfits traveled in wagons, a dozen or more — Bain's and Shuttler's, covered — strung out for miles, driving their scrub cattle and pinto ponies with them. They never lit anywhere for long, gypsying through the country like restless bands of landless Indians. Ranchers cursed when they saw them coming, for they camped anywhere the fancy struck them and never ate their own beef; the other fellow's was sweeter to their taste.

Madigan guessed maybe Jay's folks, from the way he spoke of them, were maverickers and mustangers, a notch or two farther on the illegal side than most rawhiders. He didn't ever come right out and ask, disliking inquisitiveness. He hadn't always kept too solidly on the safe side of the fence, himself.

That afternoon, riding up Hunter Creek, Jay suddenly let out a squawl and hit his horse and plunged from Madigan's sight. Madigan reined around fast, plucking out his gun, eyes searching, expecting trouble. Jay's horse hammered up one of the brushy little draws that debouched down into the creek, and Madigan heard a quick scream, a girl's scream. The hoofbeats danced to a halt. The scream pealed out again.

Madigan, spurring, put his horse around into the draw. He saw Jay hugging a struggling girl in his right arm while with his left he reined down his rearing horse. Jay must have grabbed up the girl on the run and swung her up off her feet, and he was laughing crazily at her fierce clawing and kicking. His horse, objecting, tried to unload both of them.

Madigan had seen him go headlong for

trailtown Lulus. They didn't mind; they were used to wild men wrathy for a woman. This was different.

It occurred to Madigan that Jay hadn't touched a woman since entering Texas. Most likely the hunger seethed in him and the sight of the girl had set him off. Jay's masculine urge had the straight drive of a periodic drunkard's compulsion. As recklessly excessive. It was astonishing that he should have bridled it for so long.

Madigan said, lining up his drawn gun, "Let loose of her, Jay! You crazy stallion, let her go!"

Paying Madigan no heed, oblivious of him, Jay sang out between bursts of high laughter, "Don't you know me, honey? Take a look at me! I'm your John Wesley Trubbidge!"

That actually was his name, though up north he had grown self-conscious about it and settled for Jay. People up there were apt to snicker at calling a drifting cowhand by the name of the great evangelist. He couldn't read or write, nor spell his name, and Madigan privately conjectured that Trubbidge was probably a mangled version of Trowbridge.

The girl froze rigid in Jay's arm, her face raised to his, her eyes searching him. At last she said, "Why didn't you say so? A-catchin' me thataway! Let me down, John Wesley!"

Jay, still laughing, bent over and nuzzled her pale hair. He aimed to kiss her lips, but she ducked her head. "It sure showed you don't lay out with any man what comes along, way you fought me!" he said, and then he let her down.

An out-of-line remark, that, Madigan thought. He looked for the girl to flush and run off. But she brushed her skimpy dress down with her hands, and retorted with equal bluntness, "No man ain't ever laid out with me. No man's agonna, less we marry."

"My girl!" Jay crooned.

He swung down from his saddle and stood proudly beside her. He turned a red and radiant face to Madigan. "*Amigo,* this is my own sweet Arabella! Hey, whatcha doin' with your gun out?"

"Just trying the hammer." Madigan slid the gun into his holster. "It's okay." He tried to keep his eyes off Arabella.

She *was* sweet. Blue eyes wide apart, smooth skin sunned to the color of a lightly baked biscuit. Her thin cotton dress, faded and not very clean, too obviously innocent of any bolstering of underclothes, allowed candid view of — natural growth, Madigan

21

rather sternly called it to himself. She was perhaps going on nineteen: ripe for marriage these three years or more.

He swept off his hat and bobbed his head to her. Behind the stiff bow pushed a truant thought of green hills found. He refused it, angrily condemning its source: a rage of desire, woman-hunger, inspired by the sudden appearance of a ripe young girl scantily garbed. Jay's girl.

"Glad to meet you," he said, cool and stiff.

Her eyes delved into his. She asked him, "Who are you?"

"He's a damyankee," Jay answered for him, "but mah good friend, regardless."

She paid Jay no attention. Her eyes stayed on Madigan, with a strangely grave querying as if she felt that she had known him before and ought to remember who he was. He said to her, "I'm Jim Madigan — from Idaho, way north."

Her lips moved, silently repeating his name. Then she said, putting out her hand, "Hahdy, Jim Madigan! I —"

"Where's the folks, honey?" Jay broke in.

"Up the creek a piece," she told him, still gazing at Madigan. "We been here a right long spell this time — 'bout forty days — 'count of Uncle Mark keeps sick'nin'. Jim Madigan, you got a woman someplace?"

Disturbed and uncomfortable, Madigan shook his head. He said to Jay, "We better get along to your folks."

Jay put his arms around Arabella from behind, cuddling her to him, saying, "Sure glad I run into you first! It's a good sign. What was you doin' here?"

"Pickin' greens. You made me drop 'em."

"Let 'em go. C'mon, git on my horse . . ."

Jim Madigan had lived with Shoshones, with Mexican vaqueros, and once with a band of half-breed Slota traders from Canada. He had seen rawhiders and their camps.

Never in his life had he known any people, red or white or brown, who quite matched Jay's folks. It was a new experience. Ordinarily he would have relished it and laid himself out to be one of the bunch. But one of the obstacles here was that any time he looked around he looked into Arabella's eyes.

The clan, he found, consisted of several families, but in the course of generations — God knew how many; they didn't — they had intermarried and all called themselves Trubbidge. They were fair-haired and blue-eyed, every last one of them, and some of their antiquated turns of speech hinted that their forebears might have originally emigrated westward from the mountains of Tennessee or the Carolinas — an isolated people who had retained their old identity in a new country simply because they distrusted foreign ways, and passed the distrust on to their descendants. They must have owned land once, long ago. Landless now, they kept on trundling about as if the act of migration had become an end in itself, a tradition. But they called themselves Texans, and maybe someday their momentum would run out and they would settle down.

They were wild in an earthy, half-primitive fashion. The men never shaved. The women let their hair grow long like bronco manes. Children scampered almost naked. Practically everyone over ten years old chewed pigtail-twist tobacco. Soap was a rarity, Madigan noted.

He also noted how they used rawhide in a thousand ways. It cost nothing to kill a steer if you didn't own it. Cut in long whangs, the hide spliced up a broken wagon tongue, wheel, or hub. It dried and shrank, hard as iron, clamping the break tight. From rawhide they made buckets, beds, chairs, shoes. Smoke it over a willow fire, work it limber, and it made lariats, shotgun chaps, vests, belts, even a hat if you took trouble enough and didn't mind its weight. It didn't take any keen intelligence to figure out why they were called rawhiders.

They lived in a collection of old Shuttler wagons, owned a gathering of scraggly ponies and mixed cattle, and they didn't farm a bean. They lived off the country, hunting, trapping, fishing, squatting anywhere until the restless spirit moved them, or they got run off by ranchers. A harum-scarum tribe.

Jay was an exception, of sorts. He had broken away and seen the world. Not, though, from any urge to acquaint himself with broader horizons. To make some money. To come back and cut a dash before Arabella, and strut before his folks.

Well, he had it. Not money, but the appearance of prosperity, which was plenty enough to satisfy him and impress them. A good horse of his own and a Frazier saddle. A repeating rifle and sixgun. Fancy clothes, stitched boots, spurs. No rawhide.

They spread him a grand welcome. From his extra saddle-bags he passed out colored candy to the kids, plug tobacco to the men, silk ribbons to the women. He had blown in his last few dollars on those gifts, two hundred miles back, and nursed them care-

25

fully along. The candy and plug tobacco had got stuck and wadded by the heat. Nobody minded.

For Arabella he had a silver watch, bought in San Antonio. He hadn't known it needed a winding key, and didn't get one, so it wasn't running, but everybody admired it. The only timepiece in the camp, possibly the first in decades. You shook it and it ticked a few times all by itself. Nobody ever told time but by the sun, anyhow.

To Jim Madigan they presented an iron reserve, especially the men. The women and children were guardedly friendly, but the men covertly studied his horse gear, his clothes, his speech, trying to size him up and place him. Madigan had a double-cinched saddle and a short rope tied fast to the horn; acceptable rigging, good in Texas and still good clear up to Montana, although these days the three-quarter rig was coming into favor among young range riders who liked the single cinch when it was set well forward so it held the saddle back where it belonged.

On the other hand, Madigan used a Spanish bridle, neat and light, studded with tiny silver conchas, a straight-shank Las Cruces bit, and a worn-down pair of California spurs. His stirrups were covered with eagle-

26

bill tapaderos, brush-country fashion, but he wore no chaps, and no brush jacket over his threadbare shirt. He carried his short carbine slung butt-forward under the left stirrup strap; its protruding butt bore scratches and scars beyond count. He looked cleaner than he needed to be, yet his hat was downright disreputable. His horse bore a brand that wasn't Texan.

These cow-country-wise rawhiders could read a rig and a brand at a glance, tell you where the rider came from, the size of his outfit, and what he was up to at the moment.

Madigan puzzled them, thereby causing stirrings of animosity and suspicion. He was so diversely and far-flung foreign. Even his personal shape-up was alien to theirs, he being large and loose-built, dark — a big brown man among medium-sized towheads. His eyes had a disturbing habit of fixing directly on anyone he spoke to, like he expected a reply right bang-quick out of the bag.

He overheard Jay say arguingly to a group of the men, "He's picked up gear from a hunnerd places. What o' that? I sweared by him, din' I? I brung him here as mah good friend! Hell dammit, Uncle Mark — !"

"Shed it, John Wesley — shed thet cuss

talk!" growled ancient Uncle Mark, pattoo-
ing tobacco juice and wringing out his off-
side mustache with crooked forefinger and
thumb. "Don't care where ye been nor what
ye done, ye don't cuss at me! I don't shine
to furriners, I said! He's a damyankee!"

So, Madigan thought, they didn't like him.
Well, neither did he like them, on the whole.
It was okay for Jay to call him a damyankee.
It was friendly. In the wet mouth of that old
coot, though, it was an insult, by the way he
said it.

You couldn't say they'd gone to seed,
exactly. No; got to be fair about that. The
stock that could still produce hot sparks like
Jay and Arabella wasn't all the way down
the hill. But they sure did nurse a mess of
narrow notions. Keeping to themselves
hadn't helped to open their minds. Nor
interbreeding. Everybody was related to
everybody else. Jay and Arabella were some
kind of cousins.

Left alone and apart, knowing they were
talking about him, the unwanted stranger,
the foreigner, Madigan's dislike of the Trubbidges increased by the minute.

He considered pulling out. But that would
shame Jay, so he unsaddled and gave his
horse a rubdown, and while he was at it,
occupying himself, Arabella came over and

28

stood watching him. Her silent presence prodded at his uneasy mood. He straightened up slowly, looking at her. She had put on a yellow sunbonnet and under its slat-stiffened hood her face looked small, shaded to soft tints, her eyes bluer.

She said gravely, "You don't like us, Jim Madigan. You're thinkin' we're no-'count."

Her directness disconcerted him. He had come prepared to like Jay's folks, and they had shut him out. "I like Jay," he said, and she nodded. "And — I like you."

She nodded once more — bowed her head in acknowledgment, rather, and then the broad hood of the sunbonnet hid her face, all but her chin and her lips. He wondered if some of the Trubbidges hadn't put her up to this, probing him, feeling him out.

"My folks ain't no-'count," her lips said defensively. To discover what her eyes might be saying, he would have had to squat down and peer up under the sunbonnet that she kept lowered. "They work. Summer, sometimes they catch jobs a-ridin' for the big outfits."

He knew the meaning. Payday riders. Work till the first payday and quit with a few dollars. He had done it himself, times he needed a small grubstake to push on over the next mountain range, the next desert.

"They horse-trade, too," she said.

And no doubt they doctored broken-down old wagons and buggies with bright paint, to palm off on gullible settlers.

"Sometimes they cut cedar posts to sell to ranchers. That's hard."

"Sure is," Madigan agreed. Hard indeed, to cut stout posts for ranchers who would string wire on them and fence you off from the waterholes.

"Up along the Guadalupe and the Pedernales, sometimes we make charcoal. Ain't no work harder'n hotter'n that."

True, so true again. You piled up about three cords of cut cedar endwise and shoveled up an earthen kiln over it and set it afire, and for smoke-choked days and nights you tended it. Then you broke the kiln, spread the charred cedar, doused it, let it cool off. You packed the charcoal into San Antonio or someplace for cookfires, hawking it for maybe forty cents a sack.

Cedar choppers, charcoal burners, horse traders, payday riders, maverickers . . . rawhiders. They worked when they had to. There, Madigan saw himself reflected in a murky mirror. The one difference was that he followed a vague vision whose realization he sought wryly and with dwindling hope. The rawhiders followed no vision; their future stretched as blank to them as their past.

Maybe they were fortunate, he thought, in their blankness of purpose, their complete lack of any ultimate destination. They lived for each day and expected nothing better tomorrow. They were free of those yearnings that heeled a cruel spur.

Arabella asked him, "What's it like up north where you come from?"

"Idaho? Part where I was raised, it's got hills and mountains and rivers." He paused, seeing it. "Good range in the big valleys. Grass. Wildflowers. Good hunting and fishing. The folks there are a little stand-offish, but —"

"Why, it sounds like here! I thought mebbe 'twas diff'ent."

He stood thinking that over. "In a way," he allowed, "I guess it does."

"What for didja come down here?" she asked.

He had to dig for an answer, one that might satisfy her. When he turned it over, it wasn't much. "I've been looking around for something," he said. "Awhile ago I started thinking maybe this was it. But there's always something wrong when you get up close."

He grew aware of a face just beyond Ara-

31

bella's shielding sunbonnet. A peaked young face, fuzz-haired and pale-lipped, with intense eyes. A fighty face. Madigan snapped to it, "You got any business with me? If not, back off! This talk is private and you're not invited!"

III

Arabella looked around and said about the youth, now back-stepping slowly, a grimy fist clutching the hilt of his sheathed knife, "Cousin Young Mark, him. He wanted I should be his woman if John Wesley didn' come back. Uncle Mark, he's stood a-willin' to marry us up any day."

"How?"

Evidently Uncle Mark's right to perform marriages had never before been questioned, for Arabella said puzzledly, "The reg'lar way. Like how he'll marry up John Wesley an' me."

"When?"

"This night, I reckon."

"You want to marry Jay? John Wesley, I mean?"

"I'm promised to him. Been promised a long time. Gotta marry up, now he's come back."

Was there anywhere such a thing, he wondered, as real liberty? These folks lived as free as birds, yet they bound themselves with their own ropes of tradition and out-worn precedent that allowed no room to change one's mind. The ruts of their wagonwheels scored no virgin soil; they followed in the ruts of last year and uncounted previous years. Their minds refused to spurn the old ruts, jump the tracks, go careening off to the unknown hazards of independence. They conformed to set patterns laid down by themselves. It was tragic and comic, and most of all it was a hideous waste of freedom.

He heard Jay talking loudly of the killed steer and the fight with the four cowpunchers. A stone jug was passing from mouth to mouth. Jay was anything but a discreet drinker; the hot crimson flared his face, and his eyes looked ready to burst.

He was laying it on, telling them what a wildcat this Jim Madigan was in a fight, any kind of a fight. Jim Madigan was his good friend, he kept telling them. Better friend no man ever had.

"Thet's how 'tis now," growled old Uncle Mark, and all voices hushed when he spoke. "It's got so —"

Jay broke in, explaining how he and Jim

Madigan had only wanted some beef to eat and bring along, and how those damn range riders had acted so unreasonable about it.

The listening men coughed rebukingly, silencing him. Then Uncle Mark's growl swelled out as if Jay's interruption had been no interruption to speak of, just the buzzing of a gnat.

"Got so ye cain't beef range cow 'thout trouble from Henry Severne an' him's likes. Country ain't what it was. What brand was on thet cow, John Wesley?"

"It was M Rafter O, vented, an' a big H 7 over it. I well 'member the M Rafter O outfit, but thet H 7 —"

"Henry Severne's cow. He's big. Kind of a new-come feller." Uncle Mark nodded his shaggy head. "Lemme tell you, young John Wesley. Cows now's wuth mebbe thutty dollars a head. Thutty whole dollars! Henry Severne an' him's likes ain't givin' 'em way no more. Catch ye beefin' a cow, they sheriff ye. Ol' days is gone," the old man said, and his misty eyes sought a faraway time. "Gone."

Madigan saw Jay rear up abruptly, stone jug in hand, and come stalking unsteadily out to him and Arabella. Cousin Young Mark tried to whisper to him. Jay brushed heedlessly past the youth and, hugged Arabella with his left arm. The rawhider men fell silent; they appeared to be paying no attention, but their heavily blank expressions gave them away.

The roughness of Jay's embrace caused Madigan an involuntary wince for the girl. Jay was drunk enough to make a raw play. It never took much drinking to put him over, he being naturally high-keyed to start with. His eyes had that glittering sparkle that so easily turned reckless and savage. He stuck the jug out to Madigan.

"Amigo Jim, you're too damn sober! Don't come up for air till I sing my song!"

"Okay," Madigan said. He could do with a drink. He swung the jug up and tipped it, not looking at Arabella, and gulped carefully. The liquor was sun-warmed. He thought it must have been flavored with chili peppers and aged a week.

Jay, no great shakes as a singer, hollered his favorite song, one that had brought him trouble a few times in northern company.

"Don't want no pardon fer what I was an'
    am —
Won't be reconstructed an' I don't give a
    damn!
Born high up the Guadalupe, raised on
    prickly pear,

35

Quar'led with alligators an' fit the grizzly
   bear!
Yee-ee-ow!"

Madigan lowered the jug at the final rebel yell, grinning at him. You couldn't help liking Jay, for all his faults and vices and his flaming temper. He was so honestly himself. A scrappy terrier of sunny disposition except when something burred him. Stick with you through hell and come out insulting you and all your damyankee breed. Paid any price for fancy clothes and geegaws that caught his eye, and didn't take care of them — maybe didn't know how — so he generally looked a bit seedy, a bit tawdry.

Jay took the jug back. He still hugged Arabella with his left arm, and his left hand moved, automatically exploring, as it did when he had hold of a Lulu in some joint. The girl twisted away, saying nothing. Cousin Young Mark's slitted eyes stabbed at all three of them.

"My turn," Jay said, opening his mouth to the jug. He shook it and nodded to the sloshing. "You lef' me some. *Muchas gracias, compadre!* Sing the one that feller fum Bandera kep' singin' all the way up to Kansas that time."

Madigan couldn't sing a note. He made

36

do with chanting, Indian fashion, and beat time on an imaginary drum.

"Wild and woolly,
Hard to curry,
Raised a pet, but gone wild —
And walked the Chisholm Trail backwards!
Ain't in no hurry —
Ain't in no sweat —
Hide out, little ones — hide out!"

Jay's chuckle drew no echoes from the rawhider men. They turned their faces and stared deliberately at Madigan after he ended the last half-dozen words. It came to him tardily that he was bigger than any of them. They were taking the foolish song as an insult, and they bristled touchily.

The concentration of animosity brought Madigan up straight and ready, like a curse flung at him. Any attempt at explanation would only make matters worse. The tuneless song was just a trail hand's humorous brag, and they knew it, but they wanted reasons for resenting him.

He watched Cousin Young Mark slide his hand to his knife, and men touch their weapons — old smoothbores, cap-and-ball pistols, single-shot rifles. They were in deadly earnest. Maybe they even condemned Jay as a kind of renegade for making friends with a damyankee and bringing him home. Jay had gone and lived around with foreigners so much he had become a halfway foreigner his own self. Him and his fancy clothes and gear.

Envy played its part, too, Madigan guessed. To them, sunk in their appalling poverty, Jay represented a swaggeringly prosperous showoff. The poor little sacks of candy and the dime plugs of tobacco and the ribbons stood for condescending charity now, since he let his big damyankee friend insult them.

Jay acted oblivious of the gathering storm. He went on chuckling and took another drink from the jug. Arabella, pulling her cotton dress straight, stood looking on at him and Madigan. A pretty enticement, she, by her own word a virgin, calculated to blind Jay to danger signals.

But Jay then slid his eyes around, left and right, and, as if suddenly cold sober, said to Madigan, "Let's go git a fat yearlin' for my weddin' supper, huh?"

"Let's go," Madigan agreed. Anything to avoid a shootout with Jay's folks.

Jay called to the hard-faced men, "How 'bout diggin' a fire ditch? Me an' Jim's goin' after H 7 beef for my weddin'!"

To Arabella he said softly, "It won't be long, honey. Make Uncle Mark fetch out the big Bible."

The chunks of hacked-up beef sizzled over the fire ditch, fat dripping into the wood coals and exploding smoky flares, sending forth a nostril-filling aroma. The tenders kept turning the chunks, making sure that each got its share of blackening smoke all over. Fat-smoke, they said, was what cooked it right.

They cooked it crisp, clear through so that there wasn't a trace or streak of pink left, before they called it done and fit to eat. Madigan called it ruined, to himself. It was young steer and should have come out tender and juicy, red at the bone. Steel skewers would have done the trick, allowing the heat to enter evenly and more quickly. This tasted to him like dry old bull, and it chewed like wood.

He unobtrusively tossed his half-eaten chunk into the brush, and murmured to Jay beside him, "Remember the cottontail that night in the Harque Hala, when we took a short whirl at gold prospecting? Sure was a change from jackrabbit."

"Sure got hongry that trip," Jay responded, gnawing a bone. "You didn' cook it. You jest warmed it on the fire, way damyankees do their beef. This is real grub, huh? Real cookin'!"

That wasn't Madigan's meaning at all. "Best I ever did eat," he lied. "Guess you feel good getting back to your own folks. Must do something for you."

"Yeah." Jay rolled a hot look at Arabella. "It sure do!"

Somebody spat a word urgently, ending on a hiss of warning. All the women instantly rose and moved toward the wagons, herding the young children before them. The men around the great cookfire sat motionless, their chomping jaws suspended, eyes shuttling. Like feasting wolves catching the scent of a hunter, Madigan thought. Jay leaned forward, high-heeled boots scraping the earth, gathering himself ready for a leap to his feet.

The flutter of a horse's cantering hoofs could be heard. The horse dropped to a walk, approaching, and presently halted close by in the darkness. A girl's voice hailed, "Hello-oo, the Trubbidge camp! I'm Dare Romedy, and I'm hungry!"

Everybody relaxed, smiling, calling a welcome to the girl, bidding her familiarly to come on and make herself to home. Plenty to eat; she'd dropped by at the right time — musta sniffed it from the Romedy camp a day's ride off. In reaction to the moment of tension, Jay kissed Arabella forcefully.

The visiting girl rode a black horse into the firelight and dismounted, announcing she had been hunting a stray horse since early morning and was starving. The Trubbidge women clustered around her, plying her with food and drink. Men took charge of her horse, giving it a rubdown. The animal was muddy; so was the girl. She wore canvas pants and a flannel shirt, no hat. Her hair, streaming down her back, was tangled with burrs and twigs, and there were dirt smears on her face.

What took Madigan's attention was that she had raven hair, not pale yellow. "Who is she?" he asked Jay.

Jay, occupied with Arabella, shrugged. "Never seen her before. Some rawhider gal, or the folks wouldn't know her."

"But she's got black hair," Madigan said, his protest influenced by all the towheads he had seen in this and other rawhider camps.

"Tha's right." Jay turned and looked at him. "Ain't no law says we can't grow hair any color under the goddam moon, is there?"

41

"None I know of," Madigan said awkwardly. But he went on looking at the girl, wondering what it was about her that made his interest leap, and after awhile she inevitably became aware of his regard.

As if instinctively gravitating to the only other dark one in the crowd, she walked around the fire ditch to him. "Hello!" she greeted him easily. Her eyes were emerald green. "You're not a Trubbidge." Nor, said her eyes, are you a rawhider.

"No," he replied to both statements, the spoken and the unspoken. "My name's Madigan."

"Northerner." Not a question; another statement.

"Right."

"And very much the outsider here! Here among the Trubbidges. Rawhiders." Now her eyes were mocking him, challenging him to deny his alienness.

It struck him that her manner of speech had altered. With the Trubbidges she spoke their language. Her behavior was like theirs. She was different with him. Poised, self-possessed, a girl able to talk with a man on equal terms.

"Very much," he admitted. In an effort to draw her out and learn about her, he said, "Not you, though. They treat you like one of their kind, another rawhider."

"It takes one to know one," she parried lightly.

"And that works both ways." He replaced his hat on his head. "As an outsider here, I'd take you for one."

"You'd be wrong! I'm an outsider, yes — but only as a rawhider is an outsider from the ordinary run of people. As I've always been."

Hoping to break through her poise, he tried another tack. He drew out a clean handkerchief, thin and ragged from many washings, and offered it to her. "Your face is dirty."

"I know." She took the handkerchief. "Thank you."

Her composure was not to be shaken. She wiped her face. Madigan wished he had proceeded to wipe it for her. It would have been a keen pleasure to follow the smooth contour of cheek to chin, to touch the smooth skin. She had full lips, a generous mouth. He let his gaze descend, while he speculated as to what she might be: a wife, somebody's woman, or — no, she surely couldn't be single and unattached, such a girl as this, among the early-mating rawhider folks.

Finished wiping her face, she gave him

back the ragged handkerchief, saying, "You think of these people as rubbish, I suppose, but are your ways so different from theirs?" His lowered look had not escaped her.

He met her eyes. "I'm human like them, if that's what you mean."

"Is that a confession or a declaration?"

"Both." On impulse he freed a burr from her hair. "I confess and declare I'm glad I'm a man. Are you glad you're a woman?"

"Yes."

"That's as it should be." Her thick hair lay soft in his hands. He untangled a twig from it, and in the surge of his manhood he dared to say, "That gives us good grounds to start from!"

Her lips curved. "You're very direct and — fast!" She drew her hair from his hands, letting it tumble down her shoulders.

"I have to be," he said. "You people are always on the move. So am I. There's no time for —"

Again, somebody uttered a sharp warning.

IV

As before, mothers and their youngsters retreated toward the wagons, and men sat like carved images. Then a voice inquired drily from the darkness, "Whose beef you eating?"

Immediately, Jay called back, "Who the hell wants to know?"

Uncle Mark spread his bony right hand below the level of his knees and flapped it downward cautioningly. Ease off, young John Wesley, his gesture said, ease off your big mouth. But Jay snarled, "Goddam you, give yer name — quick!"

Now he had his gun drawn. The cocking of the hammer sent a lean click distantly into the hush.

"Henry Severne," answered the dry voice, and the owner of it paced his horse into the light of the fire. "As damn well you know, old Mark! Who's the fighty one?"

He was big and blocky, with a florid face and coarse iron-gray hair sprouting from under his cuffed-back hat. He wore expensive clothes untidily, in the careless way of a man grown too accustomed to the best, and across his saddle he rested a fine English shotgun.

"Our young John Wesley jest got back home to us, Mr. Severne, sir," said old Uncle Mark, burying his whiskers in a deep nod after rising full length to show respect. "This is a weddin', sir. Ah hope an' trust ye'll stay fer the doin's."

"And eat my own beef?" Henry Severne laughed gustily in his throat. His eyes ranged imperiously over the camp and picked out Madigan and Jay. "Strangers in camp, eh? Same pair that stood off some of my boys today, I bet! Show me the hide of the steer you're eating! Where is it?"

Jay retorted, "Find it, goddam you!" He took it as an affront, the carrying of a ready shotgun into camp.

Uncle Mark rolled his eyes and shook his head at such young insolence. But Henry Severne laughed again, in the easy-going manner of a confident cattle baron who could as well afford tolerance as he could the loss of an occasional steer. "I reckon that clinches it! A wedding? Well, for a wedding I don't mind chipping in the beef."

"Ye allus been a pow'ful free-handed man, Mr. Severne, sir!" Uncle Mark assured him, his voice cracking nervously.

"Marry and multiply!" Henry Severne proclaimed. "That's in the Bible somewhere, ain't it?" He seemed in lusty high spirits. "I shun-piked round the marrying order, but damn me if I ain't made good on the second part!"

Uncle Mark creased a knowing smile. "By all reports, sir, you sho'ly have follered right stout the command to increase an' multiply. An' in the eyes o' the Lord, sir, I reckon the color don't hardly count. They's all His chil'n, if they's Christ'ns."

"They ain't all of 'em breeds," said Henry Severne a bit crisply. "Some are white clear through."

He heaved himself up and settled again in his saddle, easing his crotch. "For my H 7 beef you're eating, I claim the privilege to kiss the bride. Who's the fighty cub marrying?"

Uncle Mark hesitated for a moment. He mumbled, "Mah son Luke's wife's sister's gran'dotter, sir. Mah great-gran'-niece."

Henry Severne flapped a hand as if at flies. "Which one's that? You've got a slew of 'em."

"She — she's the one we — we call Arabella."

"So!" said Henry Severne softly.

In abject apology Uncle Mark said, "She been promised him these three-four years, sir."

"So!" The lines of laughter still lingered on the rancher's face. His eyes found Arabella and stared steadily at her, so probing that the girl folded her arms self-consciously over her thinly covered breasts.

He looked down at Uncle Mark, and the

old man shifted his eyes from the coldly violent stare. "Didn' 'spect young John Wesley back," Uncle Mark muttered. "Been gone so long, he — he purely slipped my mind."

Madigan dared not look at Jay, not wanting to witness his humiliation. To hear Jay tell it for a thousand miles, he was the old man's favorite, the apple of his eye, the shining hero of the whole Trubbidge clan; and Arabella only lived for his radiant return.

Too dismally clear, time and distance had gilded his memories with thick layers of enchantment.

Henry Severne said to Uncle Mark, "I've suspected you've been trying to marry her off lately, anyhow, whether he came back or not."

Madigan glanced toward Cousin Young Mark, and only then did the full meaning dawn on him. Uncle Mark's illness, Arabella had mentioned, was what held them here to this spot for forty-odd days, a lengthy stay by rawhider standards. His illness didn't explain how he had won the favor of squatting on H 7 range, using H 7 water and grass, eating H 7 beef sometimes and getting away with it.

There must have existed a private agreement — unspoken, perhaps, or only hinted at — between the cattle baron and the ailing old king of the Trubbidge rawhiders.

So that was it. Madigan wondered if Arabella knew of it. He guessed she did. Not only knew of it, but most likely forgave Uncle Mark because of his illness and his need to rest. Arabella, earthy beneath her angelic innocence, couldn't miss the meaning of the look in Henry Severne's eyes. As a man of his lusty nature grayed with years, he hadn't much left but to bellow his virility and cast about for fresh yoing women to whip his appetite. It was a notch to Uncle Mark's credit that he had managed to hang up the debt for forty-odd days while trying to get the girl safely married off to Cousin Young Mark.

Henry Severne's next remark corroborated it. "This is the first time anybody stole the fish off my hook!" he said bluntly. "It doesn't please me to lose her!"

Jay got it through his drink-hazed head then, and cursed in a rising shout, "Why you damn-to-hell ol' sonofabitch!"

Madigan leaped. He threw his left arm out, blocking Jay's gun. "Easy, Jay — take it easy!" Jay's face was the color of blood.

He saw the twin barrels of the English shotgun whirl up and around and over to blast Jay down, and with his right hand he

49

stroked his own gun from its holster. He drew a fast bead on the rancher.

"And *you* take it easy!"

Henry Severne inspected him thoroughly before tipping the shotgun skyward. He gathered up his dropped reins and spoke to Uncle Mark, not bothering to look again at Madigan and Jay.

"Bad company for you, that pair — bad for all of you! Cow thieves and gunslingers don't fit my idea of folks I tolerate camping on my range. They weren't included when I gave you leave to stay."

Uncle Mark raised his arms and his whiskers to heaven and vowed fervently, "Mr. Severne, sir — Ah swear us folks didn' go fer to run nothin' over on ye!"

"No?" Henry Severne eased down the rabbit-ear hammers of his shotgun. "You lying old pilgrim! You never aimed to pay off!" He swung his horse around. "I'll let you stay the night. Tomorrow you'll be in trespass, and I'll sheriff you. We'll dig up H 7 hides and jail you on cow-stealing charges! Be moving out tomorrow."

"Yessir. Thank ye, sir." Uncle Mark bowed his head. "We sho' didn' go fer to impose on yer gen'ros'ty. Jest stopped to rest a spell. Jest had to wait —"

"Forty-seven days," Severne said. For an

instant his eyes glinted in the firelight, touching on Arabella. "A long wait! Too long, old pilgrim, too long!"

He hit his horse and was gone.

And Dare Romedy was gone. Madigan looked for her. She had quietly slipped away with her black horse during the altercation, and for that alone Madigan hated Henry Severne. He took the loss of her harder than he had felt the loss of all illusions. She was gone back to the Romedy camp, God knew where, and would move on. He'd had too little time with her.

The quarreling broke out within a minute of Henry Severne's departure.

Uncle Mark, as impotently savage as a toothless old watchdog, loudly bedamned the prodigal John Wesley for bringing trouble home, making enemy with Mr. Severne who owned every blade of grass and drop of water from here nearly to Sanburn.

He left out any direct reference to Madigan, the damyankee intruder who'd pulled a gun on the mighty Mr. Severne. It remained for Cousin Young Mark to bring that up, shrilling abuse on Madigan, whereupon Jay hit him twice and laid him out senseless.

Then Jay turned and scorched Madigan

for blocking his shot at Severne. The raw-hider men all argued the case, some of one mind and some of another, and the women withdrew to the wagons, talking and taking sides, and youngsters howled, dogs yapped, and scrubby ponies catching the excitement snuffed and snorted and stamped.

They were all cracked, the whole kit and caboodle, in Madigan's opinion. He attempted to talk reason, and in return he got nothing but noise from all sides. How had these cross-grained, chaotic wanderers made out to live so long?

It took him some time to realize that they actually were drawing a perverse enjoyment from the squabble; it broke the dull monotony of their forty-seven-days' camping in one spot. They stretched the squabbling out endlessly with totally irrelevant accusations and stormy rebuttals which by involved contortions eventually straggled back toward relevence. By nature they were strenuous; underneath the thick coating of ambitionless laxity an inherited fierce activity struggled for expression — and found its outlet in constant travel. Their Old World forebears had possessed the venturesome vigor to sail to the New World, or the boldness to commit lawless acts that earned them exile to the penal colonies of Georgia long ago. The stock lived on.

At last Madigan got hold of Jay, pulled him out of a shouting group, and made him listen. "Jay, suppose Severne comes back tonight?"

But Jay had got hold of another jug of firewater and he was floating high. "I run that ol' goat off fer good!" he stated positively. "He ain't comin' back. He do, I'll eat him!"

"Suppose he comes back with a deputy sheriff and an H 7 posse?"

"I'll eat 'em all!"

"Keep your rifle handy, then, and your horse saddled."

"You ol' solemn son!" Jay fisted Madigan on the chest, with heavy affection. "Don' tell me y'gettin' skeery! You?"

"I feel cautious, tell you that."

"Aw, git shut o' it! Ev'thin's okay!"

"Maybe. But don't founder on the booze. You're damn near loaded now."

"Me?" Jay toed up an inch taller than his five-foot-nine in high-heeled boots. "Son, it's you's loaded! You don' talk sense!" He took a gulp from the jug and reeled off, mumbling amusedly that *he* didn't feel a blasted thing.

V

Old Uncle Mark had lied to Henry Severne when he intimated that he had already married Arabella off to John Wesley; or anyway he had given the rancher to understand that the girl was no longer available.

The wedding, such as it might be, had not yet been performed. Perhaps the ailing old man told the half-lie from his shamed wish to place the girl under convention protection — that same urge to avoid the consequences of a shoddy deal with the devil.

Yet Uncle Mark kept putting off the wedding, with one excuse after another. Jay prodded him, insisting, eager to claim his bride.

Uncle Mark was eating. Couldn't be interrupted. Needed nourishment for his failing strength, vowed he and the rawhiders. First time in a heap of days he could sit up and eat good.

He downed a bait of crisped H 7 beef, enough to feed an Indian, after which he got struck by a hard-breathing attack that laid him out for a snoring spell. Recovering sufficiently from that to eat some more beef washed down with liquor, he found that he couldn't just recollect to mind where he had stashed away the big Bible. He recommended that young John Wesley pray for light and guidance. The rawhiders nodded, some offering to join John Wesley in prayer.

On that grave injunction Jay spent no time that could be noticed. Choking mad and red as a rooster's comb, he sang out bitterly, "It's Cousin Young Mark you got picked to marry her up with, ain't it? But she's promised to me! I'm gonna have her! This night, by God, or —"

"Take it easy," Madigan urged him. How many times had he said it to him? In how many places? "You can't go fighting your own folks, Jay."

Jay glared all around, his eyes bloodshot. "Hell I can't!" He slapped out his gun and blazed two shots into the fire. "Uncle Mark — where's the big Bible?"

Evidently seeing how it was with Jay, that he teetered on the verge of berserk rage, Uncle Mark got well pretty quick and hollered precise directions. The big Bible lay in his wagon box, he said, wrapped in a blanket covered by a piece of canvas under two coyote pelts.

Jay himself went and got it, and plumped it down on the old man's lap. It was full quarto size, ornamented with embossed leather covers and brass clasps, and printed in dull lampblack ink on brown-edged paper.

It could have been printed in goldleaf Egyptian on papyrus, for all that the words conveyed to Uncle Mark. Reverently opening the ponderous volume at random, he started loudly reciting lines vaguely resembling the marriage service.

Madigan listened to Uncle Mark's bellowing, while his mind fondled memories of a quiet little church away up in Idaho. The young girls there wore starched dresses, immaculate. They wore their long hair in plaits, thick as your wrist almost, or if curly they gathered it with a ribbon tied in a huge butterfly bow at the nape of the neck. From the seat behind, you gazed at clean young female skin; you thought of how it would be to reach out and stroke it, when you should be listening to the minister. You were starting to discover that it seemed like whatever you wanted hardest was always illegal, immoral, or out of reach.

In a minute some of the rawhiders ventured to interrupt the recitation. They made bold to mention to Uncle Mark that he was somewhat previous, inasmuch as the bride wasn't present. Nor the groom, for that matter, at the moment. Jay was looking for Arabella, who had vanished during Uncle

Mark's procrastinations. Some laughter rumbled around.

Madigan moved back from the fire and stood staring down at the ground. If this sorry affair was funny, then there was comedy in rape. He had to bridle an uprise of violent wrath. He wanted suddenly to go after the searching Jay and hammer him down, beat him, smash him.

It turned out that Arabella had simply gone to bed in Grannie Prudence's wagon. Grannie put up a stiff resistance against disturbing a young girl's sleeping — the old lady resembled a hawk in her brown calico nightshirt, arms fluttering — but Jay won over her. Nobody could pretend to sleep, with his shouting at the canvas wagontop.

So Arabella stuck her fair head through the front flaps and said in a small voice, "I'll be out right away. John Wesley, you quit chewin' at Grannie Prudence, y'hear?"

Jay stepped back properly, bobbing his head to her and nearly falling over a rawhide bucket, everybody watching. And most properly he said, "Ah jest live to wait for you, honey!"

A few minutes went by while Arabella put her cotton dress back on, unseen inside the wagon. For her wedding.

And then a gunshot blared from the black night's fringe around the camp. A voice barked out of the darkness, "Freeze tight, you Trubbidges! This is the law! We're here for cow thieves and gunslingers! Goddam you, freeze up!"

Madigan whirled immediately and dived out of the firelight. He had kept his horse saddled, loose-cinched, reins tied to a forefoot, since his caution to Jay. A rifle lashed three rapid hots after him, tearing up earth. He stripped the reins loose and vaulted into the saddle; no time to haul up on the cinches.

He yelled, "Come on, Jay — it's us they want!"

Shooting exploded all around. A Trubbidge man flung away a knife, then clasped his thigh and dropped face-down. Uncle Mark tremblingly raised the big Bible high between bony hands and skinny arms, like an early Christian exhorting divine protection from the persecutors. Women screamed and youngsters bawled.

The Bible canted over and fell on Uncle Mark's head. Maybe a bullet had punched it, the shooter finding it a tempting target, not knowing what it was. Bad luck for that shooter, if he found out what he'd shot.

They wouldn't harm the women, Madigan knew for sure. The high-flown punctilio of this Texas country commanded that no woman be treated roughly, whoever and whatever she might be. To hell with the men — they were twenty times more plentiful. As for shiftless rawhider vagabonds, they never stayed in one place long enough for the men to vote and wouldn't vote if they did.

Madigan saw Jay running to the horses, bent low. It was only a glimpse, but enough; Jay hadn't taken the precaution to keep his own horse saddled. Still, one good thing about him was that although he did have the habit of getting drunk, he sobered fast in a tight scrape. Jay would make his getaway if it was at all possible. The trouble was, likely as not he'd kill somebody. In his queer set of values, life and death didn't stand at the top of the list.

A louder and more concentrated flurry of gunfire broke out — some of it for Jay, Madigan guessed, some for himself. Bullets clipped twigs from the live oak above his head. Most men shot too high in the dark. No doubt Jay was putting in a share of the shooting while forking a horse. Madigan reined around to ride there and give him a hand. Jay had done as much for him a time or two.

Then Jay screeched, "Git a-goin', Jim — I'm clear! You okay?"

"Okay!" Madigan shouted back. He half-circled his horse and heeled it plunging off up the bank of the creek. "Last night's camp, Jay — see you!"

"See you!"

It rained late that night, a furious downpour accompanied by wild scrawls of lightning and tremendous thunderclaps. The storm lasted an hour and left the ground spongy.

Madigan met Jay at their last night's campsite, around four in the morning. They both shivered.

"Have much trouble throwing 'em off?" Madigan asked.

Jay jerked a shoulder, meaning, yes, some, to hell with it. He had turned up riding bareback one of the Trubbidge ponies, and he tenderly rubbed his sore backside. His mood was low.

Madigan said, to fire him up, "I sure like the Texas you pranced so gay about. What I admire is that freehanded hospitality to the stranger and the weary wayfarer. It gets me. Everybody here's our friend. They just can't do enough for us."

It failed his purpose. Jay hung his head. "Man, don' rub it in! You know how I feel."

Madigan nodded, charity having its way. "I do."

They rubbed their horses down. Madigan laced his saddle on again, and said, "You'll be wanting to prowl back to Hunter Creek, I guess. For your horse and saddle. And your rifle. We better go *cuidado.* That H 7 posse might be on the hunt for us still."

"Yeah," Jay muttered. "Gotta git my wife, too."

"Wife?" Madigan's tone was sharper than he intended. "You didn't get to marry Arabella last night. You only nearly did."

"Near as makes no odds. Uncle Mark, he preached out near all the words from the big Bible."

"He wasn't reading from it," Madigan said impatiently, "nor from any Bible ever written! He's not qualified to perform marriages. Furthermore, Arabella wasn't even present. She's no more your wife than she is mine."

Jay's eyes glimmered strangely. He said with chill and stilted politeness, "I ain't requirin' you should go back with me. You didn' lose nothin' there. Didn' leave nothin' o' yours behind. Did you?"

Madigan thought it over. "That's right, I didn't." He was able this time to keep his

61

tone neutral. "But I guess I'll go back with you."

Jay looked hard at him. In the semidarkness of pre-dawn neither one could read the other's expression and thoughts very well. At last Jay said shortly, "Okay."

They rested their mounts a spell first, Jay's pony needed it, having been ridden hard in throwing off the H 7 men, and lacking the stamina of Madigan's horse. Madigan had got away on a fast start and taken it fairly easy thereafter. That made the saving difference between a good grain-fed horse and a grass-fed scrub. It was the difference, too, between foresight and carelessness. Poor folks and careless folks paid highest in the end.

Sometimes, when tolerance slept, Madigan thought poverty and misfortune were too often the bedraggled sisters of carelessness. But that, awakened tolerance protested, ignored the mischances that met a person unexpectedly. Life was rarely a simple matter. An act by someone you never knew could foul up all your calculations. So, said tolerance, you gave a helping hand to the man in trouble.

Madigan and Jay stood together in the mud, saying nothing while their horses cropped the rain-wet grass. The early dawn brightened to sunlight, trees flaring bright green, scarlet cardinals winging about and scolding: *"Pee-quew, pee-quew — tut, tut, tut!"*

A bluejay flashed across a cardinal's soaring path, brilliant cobalt, and for that instant it seemed to Madigan that the vibration of opposed colors shimmered the whole sky. Below, a meadow shone, rain-heavy cottonwoods dripping diamonds. Depravity and violence were as remote as last night's stars.

"We better start," he said; and Jay muttered, "Yeah."

Those were the last words of any importance they spoke all the way back to within sight of Hunter Creek. Something prickled between them, making them uneasily taciturn. They would not mention it, but both had a keen awareness of its dangerous presence. Rather than risk letting out an unguarded word, they held talk down to a minimum, thinking before speaking.

"Them H 7 buzzards must be quit."

"We won't bank on it."

Another half-mile, and — "They'd shoot now if they was there."

"They're gone."

And gone also were the rawhiders, with their patched-up wagons, shaggy ponies, scraggly cattle, uncombed women and half-wild youngsters. The sheltered draw contained only some bare spots, blackened campfire spaces, the fire ditch, and wheel tracks.

"Reckon they'll head over to the Pecos," Jay said. "Or Charcoal City, if they's broke. Or mebbe —"

His musing eyes flicked to a patch of low oak and shortleaf pine, and fastened there. His gun came up and he snapped flatly, "Come out o' thet, Cousin Young Mark, 'fore I shoot your front teeth out!"

His eyesight had often amazed Madigan. It amounted to more than sight; it edged on an animal sensitivity.

Cousin Young Mark came pushing out into the open, riding Jay's saddled horse, carrying Jay's repeating rifle. His peaked young face twitched, its fighty streak struggling against fear.

Wickedly polite, Jay purred, "Ah sho' thankee kin'ly for gath'rin' up mah b'longin's, sonny! Do the same for you, if you live that long. Where-at's the folks gone?"

Cousin Young Mark grated in high key, "No'th."

Jay raised an eyebrow. "Wha'for? Yer a liar,

sonny! Gimme it straight — where-at's they gone?"

"Damn ye!" shrilled the youth. "Goddam ye to hell, John Wesley!" He jerked up the rifle clumsily, not used to it.

Jay covered him dead center between the eyes with his gun, saying, "Kill me for mah rifle an' horse an' woman, wouldja?"

The killing impulse weakened and died, smothered by the cruel inferiority of an untried stripling facing a seasoned man. "She ain't your woman!" Cousin Young Mark snarled, and with the tedious profanity of the unlearned he told of what had happened.

Henry Severne's range boss — who, it turned out, also was conveniently a deputy sheriff — had arrested the whole Trubbidge tribe for cattle theft, upon returning from the chase with his H 7 posse. He had asked Henry Severne what he wanted to do with them, and Severne said he wanted them jailed and their trespassing wagons burned where they stood.

That was, Severne amended, shushing the clamoring Trubbidges, unless old Uncle Mark could offer a guarantee against their doing further mischief on H 7 range.

Uncle Mark got the hint, bowed to the

inevitable, and when the heehawing ended it was solemnly declared that Arabella had agreed to post herself as a living bond — a hostage, as it were — for all her folks.

Off she went on an H 7 horse, in her cotton dress, bare legs showing. Henry Severne rode beside her, as her proprietor or protector — or anyhow as a kind of appointed guardian. His range boss, the deputy sheriff, dropped back to mention to the Trubbidges that it would be best for all concerned if they rolled on out of the country while they had the chance. The girl would be set free to follow them when they were gone, no harm done.

It was a sordidly unlawful piece of business, but for the rawhiders the law was always on the side of the other fellow. Having no more standing than a band of tramps, they hastily pulled out. Maybe they believed the deputy sheriff. Maybe.

You couldn't tell about them, Madigan thought. They were so simple in most ways, so primitive. You had to be charitable, or you fell into narrow errors of judgment. They were irresponsible and none too honest, yet not actually evil.

Yes, Cousin Young Mark answered to Jay's crackling question, Arabella sure was at H 7 headquarters on Upper Johnson Creek. She was the house guest — Cousin Young Mark used an odd term, *house lady* — of Henry Severne. Since sunup.

Jay said to him, "Git off mah horse! Gimme mah rifle!" He spoke in a thin, pinched treble. "Quick!"

The youth obeyed him. He swapped for Jay's played-out pony and handed over the repeating rifle. He slid his leg over the pony and took off, thumping its ribs with his rawhide shoes.

Jay sprang into the saddle, whispering curses, panting, his eyes starting from his crimson face. He fumbled with the rifle, nearly dropped it, and rubbed savagely at his left arm; once in a while he had complained that it went numb on him, blaming it on those freezing winters up north.

Madigan said to him, "Get your hackles down, will you? This could be on the square, to make sure your folks quit. Severne can't just take a girl and —"

"Hell he can't! You seen how he eyed her!"

"Sure — but *she's* straight, I'd swear. She —"

"All the more reason! You don't know what I know!"

Madigan frowned. He demanded, "What's that mean?"

Jay trembled under the strain of his pas-

67

sion. "All them women — Dodge, Denver, Cheyenne, Tombstone — ev'ry damn place I been. They was innocent young girls once, like Arabella!" he declared, his eyes tragic. "Got betrayed by some man, ev'ry last one of 'em. They done tol' me. Wine an' false words — an' worse! An' then a life o' shame!"

This, Madigan thought, was comedy: a country boy whose superior knowledge of women had been purchased from cribjoint trulls who told him the routine tale, the teary story of downfall given to any gullible yahoo for another drink, another dollar.

"It could be a trick to bait you in," he said. "Severne thinks you married her. He wants you put out of the way. A man will take long chances to get his bride back."

"My bride!" Jay stared at nothing. "No, no, I'd kill her first! Be better for her! That kind o' shameful life? Goddam — not her! Not my Arabella!"

And what he meant was, Madigan thought, not *him* — he couldn't bear knowing that Arabella was possessed by another man. Ravished and debauched. Male ego raised raging protest.

"Let's go after her!" Madigan said. A harsh urgency edged his voice, for he found that he felt much the same way about it.

68

"I ain't requiring you should —" Jay began in his thinnest, meanest tone.

"Damn your piddling soul, quit balking and let's go get her!" Madigan roared, and Jay put heels to his horse.

VI

In constructing his home Henry Severne had departed from custom and adopted architectural features not usually incorporated in a Texas ranch house. It was a half-timbered building, much the same style as of the houses of prosperous and large-familied German settlers north of San Antonio: massive uprights and cross-beams of squared cedar, the gaps solidly filled with rock and mortar. A heavily imposing house.

However, he had mitigated its severity by adding on the Spanish flourish of an open portico, wide and flagstoned, with a sloping roof that shaded colorful splashes of painted Mexican chairs and tables, and bright Indian rugs and hanging *ollas* from the Navajo country. Four doors faced out onto the portico; all four hung wide open.

A long and comfortable-looking bunk-house, with cook house attached, stood a respectable distance to the rear. Farther back, the outbuildings and corrals and pens fanned out spaciously.

Anyone could see that the H 7 was a kingpin outfit, probably the biggest in a day's ride, owned by a man who could well afford to live generously — as no doubt he did, except when driving a bargain for what he wanted: more land, cattle, horses, another woman. He couldn't have acquired all this by bighearted negligence, at a time when other cattlemen were only beginning to prosper.

It lay on high ground. A stream ran south below the corrals. North, fronting the big house and its portico, grassed land swept up clear and open to a grove of pecan trees, and above the pecans the Sanburn stage road bent past. A carriage driveway had been cut through the grove, curving from the road to the house. A gracious Southern touch, that, mutely inviting stage coaches to pull in for rest and hospitality. Among the fares there might be a pretty woman, one who could be induced to dally a while with the cattle baron who allowed the stage road to cross his range.

The thick foliage of the pecans screened Madigan and Jay from sight of the house. Nor could they see much after entering the grove, and no sounds reached them.

"That saddle of yours creaks like a new boardwalk," Madigan muttered to Jay. "Never noticed it before. Wonder if things are always this quiet around here?"

"It's quiet, all right. Can't hear nothin'." Jay pressed a fist to his chest and made as if to belch, but no belch came.

"Outfit this size, should be somebody doing something, if it's only whistling." Madigan glanced toward the sun-glare through the trees. "Ought to hear the cook banging his supper pans."

"Reckon they's listenin' for us?"

"I still think it could be a trick to bait you in."

"An' you!"

"Both of us, yeah. They can shoot us on sight, saying we're in trespass, out of law, and up to no good. All they have to do is wait for us to show ourselves."

"They" — Jay gulped a breath — "ain't got long to wait!"

"Severne won't be wanting us alive to tell it around Sanburn that he forced a young girl to live with him," Madigan said, laying it out straight, trying to reach Jay's common sense. "And his riders hold a grudge against us. We could wait till dark."

"Not me!"

"No, I guess you can't."

Their eyes met, and now they were close again, right bower to sidekick and all friction laid aside. Madigan said, "Well?" And Jay echoed, "Well?"

"We tie our horses here. We ease on down there, keeping to the trees. Bring your rifle."

As they descended through the pecan grove the foliage rose above them, until, peering around the trunks, they could see all of the H 7 headquarters — the main house and its grand portico, and the long bunkhouse and well-built outbuildings.

Then, near the edge of the grove, Jay uttered a wrenching grunt as if punched in the stomach and too hurt to curse. He stood stock-still, staring at the girl on the portico.

Arabella sat there on a painted chair by a little painted table. She wore a dress of rose-colored velvet embroidered with gold thread, tight-fitting in the bodice, the skirt flowing full, the kind of dress never seen in a rawhider camp and rarely on a ranch. She had done something to her pale hair; it was piled up regally on her head and looped with a silk ribbon. While Madigan and Jay watched her, she raised a long-stemmed glass from the table and took a sip of red wine. A ring flashed on her finger.

Setting down the wineglass, she rested

back in the chair and raised a hand to her hair, causing her breasts to strain prominently at the tight bodice. In that pose she reminded Madigan of a St. Louis woman he had known for an expensive hour.

They did learn fast. Or perhaps they knew the soft tricks by feminine instinct, and only needed a break in the fence to cut loose and cavort. Still, even so, this was mighty prompt and fast a jump for a rawhider girl. From simple virgin to elegant mistress, within the space of a few hours. It surely beat the record. It raised doubts.

Madigan turned his mind to considering how to reach the portico alive. The expanse of grass between it and the pecan grove offered no cover whatever. He spoke quietly to Jay.

"Look — I'll get my horse and pull back to the road, and I'll come riding easy down that carriage path to the house. They didn't get too good a look at my face last night. If I drift in like a saddle tramp sniffing for supper, maybe nobody'll pay me much notice. You stay here and cover for me. I'll come out a hell-sight quicker'n I went in, and I'll have her along."

He took Jay's incoherent growl as a protest against his carrying the most risk, and in rebuttal he said, "You're a better shot with that rifle than I am. You know it. Watch those four open doors, eh?"

He started back to his horse. It occurred to him that Jay had failed to answer, and he swung around. "You'll cover for me, won't you, Jay?" he called low-voiced. "Hey — wake up, blast you! I've got to be sure!"

Jay made no response to that, either. From where Madigan had halted he could see Jay's left profile, lighted by a ray of the lowering sun. Jay's left eye was round and wide, weirdly like old Uncle Mark's eyes above the big Bible, burning with the positive conviction of his own rightness. But Jay's mouth twisted painfully; he raised his rifle.

"Jay!" Madigan whispered.

Shouldering the butt of the rifle, Jay laid his cheek to it. Now he was sobbing. His blood-congested face streamed sweat. He blinked fiercely to clear his eyes, and steadied the rifle by resting its barrel and his left forearm against the trunk of a pecan tree. Nothing living existed in sight down there for him to shoot at, except the girl.

"Jay!"

Blinking again, tears and sweat filling his eyes, and his hard-panting breath shaking him, Jay had obstacles to overcome in fulfilling his self-imposed duty. Madigan saw him swallow a breath and hold it, giving himself the needed moment of steadiness in which to sight the rifle. He sighted it at the rose-colored dress, ever so carefully.

Madigan whipped out his gun, cocked it, swung it up level in one unbroken movement. "Jay!" he called desperately. "Quit that! I'll drop you, Jay! You hear me?"

Jay didn't hear; or if he did, the plain warning made no dent in his somber passion. He was beyond heeding anything outside of the task in hand: merciful execution of the girl he loved. His concentrated care meant that he was aiming for a heart shot, for a clean kill that would not let her suffer. His finger moved on the trigger, taking up the first gentle pressure, then pausing for the shaved instant of final certainty before the shot.

Madigan fired.

The echoes of the shot rattled briefly off the front of the house, and silence returned. Eerily, the big outfit showed no more sign of life than before. Arabella rose swiftly from her chair, but that was to be expected. That was all; she didn't come forward out of the shaded portico, but just stood there gazing toward the pecan grove.

Jay raised his bullet-shattered left hand. He stared from it to Madigan. It had taken a bullet to penetrate his consciousness, and mercy had kept Madigan from killing him, but with his awakening came an explosive rage of frustration.

"Jim! You — you — !"

His face contorted, hardly recognizable, mouth gaping wide, eyes rolling. His whole body jerked up rigid. He touched his bloodied hand to his chest. Something like a groan came from him and he fell face down.

Madigan ran to him, knelt and rolled him over. He had learned what to do when Jay, under stress, threw a fit.

But Jay wasn't breathing. His heart wasn't thumping. This wasn't another fit. This was death. Jay's trouble hadn't been in his stomach. Madigan had guessed it was higher up, and thought so did Jay, sometimes; but Jay would never admit it as long as he could lay his trouble to damyankee cooking.

There was nothing to be done for him, no time to spend on sentiment or regret. Madigan left him lying in the pecan grove, and started his dash to the house.

Sprinting down the grassy slope, he got a dismaying feeling that Arabella and the whole H 7 outfit were silently laughing at him, regarding his intrusion as a foolish impertinence not worth serious consideration.

Furious, he halted so abruptly that his high heels plowed the damp topsoil and caused him to teeter awkwardly. He caught his balance and stood half crouched, his eyes shuttling rapidly from one to another of the four open doors. The doors gaped a blankness of shadowy interior that could be active and yet be blinded from him, for the low sun was on him and made all shadowed objects black before his eyes.

He called to Arabella roughly, "Come here to me! Quick!" And she didn't move. Her face to him became a pale, calm blur, a shaded mask.

For the first time in his life he swore at a woman. He cursed her in the bitter terms Jay should have had the right to use. She remained unmoving. Her blue eyes, fastened on his, were strangely intent. He thought she was taking in his cursing, then suddenly sensed that she was not. She was listening to something else, and her eyes were trying to convey a message to him.

A figure stepped out onto the portico, quietly, unhurriedly. Henry Severne.

The door that Severne emerged from was the one almost directly behind Arabella. He wore dark clothes, inconspicuous in shadow.

77

The table and chairs and the girl provided him some cover. He had the gall to step out alone, but not the young pride to offer an even break. While hedging his act with every precaution short of ringing in his crew, he would plume his middle-aged vanity by making the motion of meeting an enemy face to face in the presence of the girl.

"By God, you did show up, sure enough!" he drawled. The girl was too small to shield all of his blocky frame, so he kept to the width of the portico behind her. "She made bet you would. If you didn't, she said, she'd come to me willing. Not that I mind a girl's willing or not, but I took the bet. Where's your partner?"

"He's dead," Madigan said. "Back there in the grove."

"You killed him? That shot —"

"Only shot him through his hand. It was his heart that gave out. I'll have to leave it to you to bury him."

"Sure. We don't leave our dead above-ground around here. Do the same for you." Severne's tone was dry, confident. "*Bien venido,* pilgrim! That means 'good welcome' in Mexican."

"*Sabe,*" Madigan said, waiting.

"Oh, yeah — your name's Madigan, they told me. Used to live in these parts. I've

78

heard about the Mad Madigans." Severne laughed, a deep hu-hu-hu sound. "*Sabe 'adios'?* Means 'goodbye'!" He raised his fine English shotgun, and then he had to shift a bit to line it up past Arabella.

Madigan said, "*Sabe, cabron!*" He cut loose a shot at once.

His bullet flayed chips from the carved stock of the expensive shotgun. It did no other harm than to knock the shotgun up and aside a few inches, so that the first blast flashed high and tore a hole in the edge of the portico's sloping roof.

Arabella stood motionless between them. Madigan's bullet had skimmed over her shoulder by a hand's breadth. She didn't duck, nor scream, but just stood there watching Madigan's eyes.

The shotgun swerved down to make score with the second barrel. Madigan poked his gun out at arm's length and lined up the coarse sights — a recourse that he, a snap-shooter, seldom took.

Severne's years of woman-hunting dissipation had not softened his nerve, whatever it had done to his morals. In the pinch he was a tough man. He weaved from side to side of Arabella, smiling, watching for his opportunity. The thing could have been a neighborly turkey shoot, it was so unexcited, unflurried.

Arabella moved. She took only a short sidestep. It brought her head in front of the shotgun's muzzle, blinding it and Severne's face from Madigan's sight. She must have known her peril of getting her head blown off, yet her eyes expressed only that cool intentness, watching Madigan's eyes, watching the shift of them, reading from them the moves of Severne behind her. Rawhiders learned many tricks at an early age.

Henry Severne, on the point of firing, moved to clear his aim. Again Arabella moved, this time a full step aside. If she'd had eyes in the back of her head she couldn't have timed it better. She left Severne fully exposed, and Madigan got off a swift shot at him.

The shotgun roared its second charge low into the painted table and chairs. The table toppled on three legs and Severne stumbled into it, grasping his right arm and shouting for his crew to come out and get the gun-slinging bastard.

Madigan started to command Arabella to get a move on, but she was already running to him, holding up the long skirt of her dress. He caught his arm around her and they raced for the grove, hearing the H 7 men piling out of the bunkhouse.

VII

"You're awful solemn," Arabella said, late that night. "You frettin' 'count o' me?"

A hungry camp by a waterhole at the end of a hard ride, and she was concerned only about what he thought of her. He marveled at her singlemindedness. She must know that the horse she had ridden straddle in her gorgeous dress was Jay's, but she wouldn't speak of it.

"It's true what he said — Henry Severne. I bet him you'd come for me, you an' — an' John Wesley." She sat on the ground, hands clasped around her knees. "If you didn' come by sundown, I said, I'd lay with him. But I knowed you'd come, Jim, I jest knowed it."

"Sure," Madigan said. "You bet right."

He lay stretched with his head pillowed against his saddle, worn out, but too restless to let go and get some sleep. His thoughts refused to detach themselves from Jay, left dead in the pecan grove. He tried to line up the course ahead, with rigid forethought.

Trace the Trubbidge wagons. Take Arabella back to her folks. No; they'd fear the wrath of Henry Severne following them. Rightly so. Severne would look for her there and find a way of forcing her back to him, if only to pay off his score and mend his damaged self-esteem.

Take her far off, then, out of Texas. But that involved too much of a — well, first off, a man traveling with a young girl companion . . .

The thought intruded: I'll never make another friend. I'll never dare, after Jay. And I want nothing more to do with rawhiders. Not this girl. Not even Dare Romedy.

The memory of Dare Romedy hit him keenly. Her emerald eyes and curving lips, her voice, her thick black hair soft in his hands. The manner of her walk. The wild enticement of her near presence. But she had slipped away, God knew where. She was another rawhider. Another mirage, withdrawing its warm, unspoken promise before he had scarcely begun to reach toward the glory of its fulfillment.

"Where we goin'?" Arabella asked him. "Not no'th, Jim. I wouldn't like it up there, all cold, an' the folks cold too. I don' wanna leave Texas."

That, he mused, narrowed the problem a bit. Texas it had to be, for her. A hot climate and hotblooded people; too hot at times.

"All right," he said tiredly. "I'll think of something by morning."

"You goin' to sleep now?"

"I'm going to try. You better, too."

"I ain't sleepy a speck," she declared, "but I'll lay down by you, you want."

He fought off the wanting. "You sleep where you are," he told her. "Didn't you say you'd never lay with a man unless you're married to him?"

"I reckon we be same's married, we stay t'gether," she countered reasonably.

He conceded that probability, at the same time shying away from the prospect. To save her pride, he said, "It's best not to rush into anything you might be sorry for later. G'night, Arabella."

Just before dropping off to sleep he heard her murmur, "I reckon it's 'cause you're from the no'th."

In the morning he found that she had taken off the velvet dress and carefully folded it. Severne, she told him, had provided it and other articles, ordering her to get dressed up like a lady. From her description, Severne evidently kept a cozy guest chamber equipped with feminine apparel and accoutrements ready in reserve for eventualities. A Mexican housekeeper had fixed up Arabella's hair.

However, constrained by some kind of moral qualm — it couldn't have been fastidiousness — Arabella had balked at clothing herself from the skin out in Severne's gifts, even in privacy. And not for an instant would she consider the hot bath prepared for her — "Not in *his* house I wasn't takin' no bath!"

She had merely slipped the velvet dress on over her own cotton one, which she was wearing now.

In the bright morning sunshine the thin cotton dress was not only immodestly revealing, it was drab and soiled. Such washings as it had undergone had perhaps consisted of dunking it in a stream and wringing it out. Arabella had also taken off the shoes that went with the velvet dress. Compared to the elegant girl on the portico, she looked like a ragged waif — which, Madigan reflected, wasn't far from the truth.

Something had to be done about it. He gave a modicum of credit to Henry Severne for having at least had the grace to improve the girl's appearance. Too bad she hadn't taken full advantage of the facilities offered her. That hot bath, for one thing . . .

He said gently to her, "I guess it wouldn't

84

bother the cows if you washed in the water-hole. I'll keep my back turned."

She wasn't disturbed about his back. "You mean go right in an wash all over? It's jest my feet's dirty."

"Might as well make a bath of it. Could wash your dress, too, and, uh, your under-clothes. I've got soap."

Her eyes rounded. "I ain't got no underclo'es!"

"Hm!" Just that one skimpy piece of worn-out garment, and nothing more. As he had guessed. "Why don't you throw that dress away and put the other one back on?"

"It's too good to wear ridin'." She stroked the rich velvet. "But if you want me to —"

"It'd be nice. We're going in to Sanburn." He paused, shaping words to introduce gradually to her the possible solution to his problem that had occurred to him during the night. "I'll be taking you to meet a lady who's apt to judge by appearances."

Arabella's eyes sharpened. "Is she young an' purty?"

"No, she's getting on in years, old enough to be your mother. Older." And I only hope she's still there, he thought. I hope she'll remember me.

"Oh. A' right, I'll wear it." Arabella began unfolding the velvet dress.

85

"You'll want to wash first." He dug out his bar of soap and gave it to her.

She took it and walked to the waterhole, shaking her head in amusement. "John Wesley *said* you was hell on washin'!"

"So's the lady I'm taking you to meet. Her name's Miss Osborne. She's from Louisiana. Used to teach school in New Orleans. Private school, I think."

He watched her wade into the waterhole, soap in hand. Without looking around, she started drawing the cotton dress off over her head, and he quickly turned his back.

It was astonishing that she should have retained her virtue among the half-wild rawhider lads. Still, maybe not. For all their wildness, rawhiders took a sternly unforgiving view toward promiscuity. Notwithstanding their loose forms of marriage, they were downright prudish. Old Uncle Mark, making his shoddy bargain with Henry Severne, was an exception — and he had done his best to welsh on it.

The parlor of the Osborne residence testified to the genteel background of Miss Sibyl Osborne and her brother, Dr. Edward K. Osborne. Lace curtains over the windows restrained the sunlight from fading the wallpaper, and thick draperies could be

86

drawn to muffle the noises of Sanburn's main street. Gilt picture frames glinted darkly in half-lighted corners. A marble-topped table held a massive brass lamp that was shaded under a smother of bunched silk and artificial flowers. Rugs tripped the unwary feet.

It awed Arabella tongue-tied, which Madigan counted as fortunate. First impressions were important. She stood a fair chance to pass the test, if she kept quiet.

Her attire made her appear not too out-of-place in the parlor, and she wore it well, her feminine instinct quick to take advantage of finery. In fact she was far more richly garbed than Miss Sibyl, if not as appropriately for the time of day. Madigan was glad he had made her wear the dress, although riding into town it had drawn stares. A girl in ballroom raiment of rose velvet and gold trimmings, riding horseback under the midday sun, wasn't a common sight anywhere. And many of the staring men had recognized him, Madigan knew, when they were able to wrench their eyes off Arabella. Their expressions had changed from startled wonder to displeasure.

"Perhaps," Miss Sibyl suggested with stilted delicacy to Arabella, "you desire to wash your hands?"

Arabella obediently stood up, looking at her hands in surprise and then at the elderly spinster.

"Come this way, my dear."

Arabella's face told Madigan that she was beginning to feel surrounded by soap fanatics. Left alone with Dr. Osborne, he said awkwardly, "She's a good girl, Doctor," hoping for a man-to-man talk that would straighten out matters.

Ignoring the hint, Dr. Osborne crossed the room to adjust an elaborately framed picture by a fraction of an inch. His lack of response was characteristic of him; he combined aloofness with stiff formality. Nobody ever dared to call him Doc. Even his wife had addressed him by his title. After she died, leaving him a childless widower, his sister had come to keep house for him, bringing with her the family treasures from New Orleans and a rigid decorum accrued from heading a private school for select young ladies.

The Osbornes made no friendships, nor entered into the social life of Sanburn. The town was proud of them — Southern gentry of the genuine stock, all agreed, as anyone could see. Dr. Edward Kendall Osborne, short, erect, unfailingly correct in manner and dress, commanded respect. Men tipped their hats to him as he passed by in his buggy. Miss Sibyl, tall by contrast, pale and stately, could quench the slightest familiarity with a glance.

Having discreetly maneuvered Arabella out of the room, Miss Sibyl returned to her wicker chair and asked Madigan quietly, "Why did you bring her here?"

He became aware of voices outside in the main street. Shifting his chair, through a curtained window he made out two men standing in front of the house. Two badges winked in the sunshine. So the word had already gone out.

"I didn't know of a better place for her," he answered. "Fact is, I can't think of any other place if you don't take her in." He paused. "She's too young to go it alone."

"You mentioned that she has broken away from her own people — that they have moved elsewhere. Rawhiders, I think you called them?"

"Yes." Not being cow folks, the Osbornes didn't hold any prejudice against rawhiders. They had only the vaguest idea of what rawhiders were. "They're sort of drifters," he said. "She deserves a better life. I think she'd learn fast."

"Possibly. Her facial structure does indicate a degree of intelligence. I have not really heard her voice, so I cannot judge her diction. Has she had schooling? How well does she know her letters and figures?"

"She can read cattle brands," Madigan hedged.

"That, one supposes, is a beginning," Miss Sibyl rather drily, observed, while something like a flicker of challenge lit up her aging eyes. The inveterate teacher's instinct to teach. "Tell me, please" — she cleared her throat — "what precisely is your relationship to her?"

"Let's say I just happened along at the right time to help her. She was homeless, penniless."

"She appears rather overdressed, for a girl who is destitute!"

It's a good thing, Madigan thought, you didn't see her before, underdressed in that cotton rag. He said nothing.

Dr. Osborne spoke up. "You're leaving out several facts and details, aren't you, Madigan?"

Madigan looked at him, knowing by his cold tone that he was in opposition. "You're right, Doctor," he said. "But what I leave out is nothing you need to know. It's for her to tell you, if she wants to. There's nothing in it for her to be ashamed of. Nor me."

"I am inclined to accept that, Edward,"

Miss Sibyl told her brother. "I remember the Madigan young men as wild, most terribly wild —"

"They were all patients of mine at one time or another, Sibyl. Gunshot wounds, usually. And they made other patients for me. You have no need to remind me of the Madigans!"

"Quite so. Deplorable. But immorality" — she stressed the word — "was not known to have a part in their vices. Their manner toward me was at all times most respectful."

Dr. Osborne eyed her sharply. "Does this mean that you actually favor taking that girl into our home? An unknown girl of heaven only knows what background? I am against it! You astonish me, Sibyl!"

"Edward," she replied firmly, "it taxes me to maintain this house in proper order. You must remember that I am no longer young, nor overly strong. The girl can be a help to me. In return, I can instruct her in many ways. The domestic arts. Social graces." Her eyes shone. "Speech and deportment. All the essential —"

"After a lifetime of teaching, I should have thought you'd had enough!"

"On the contrary; I miss it. To educate is to uplift. Teaching is as noble a profession as healing."

"I grant that with reservations." The doctor paused to straighten another picture a hair's breadth, before turning to Madigan. "If we take the girl in at all, I insist that it be only on trial. A probationary period. If there is dissatisfaction, out she must go!"

Madigan shook his head. "I can't go off knowing she might get thrown out after I'm gone!"

"Indeed!" said the doctor. "Indeed! Quite a high-minded sentiment, I'm sure. You came here with a purpose. Your purpose was to load your reponsibility onto my sister, who is not in the best of health, leaving you free to go your way! How typical of the Madigan brothers!"

Madigan flushed. "Guess I earned that," he acknowledged, thereby confessing that he had at least hoped to accomplish some such purpose.

Miss Sibyl made to speak, but Dr. Osborne forestalled her, saying acidly, "It would seem that a sense of duty was left out of the Madigan makeup!"

"That remark's not called for." Madigan kept his tone level, but his civility was slipping and the continued presence of the two lawmen out front ruffled him. "I feel a certain amount of responsibility for Arabella — a common duty to help her because she needs helping. Otherwise I wouldn't have brought her here, with my hat in my hand, begging you to take her in!"

"I suppose it was the best you could do."

"It was. I don't feel duty bound to spend the rest of my life looking after her. I can't do it, a man my kind."

"So you expect us to do it for you!"

Madigan drew a breath, and then he let loose. "I did expect you to see your common duty, as I saw mine! For me? No! For her. For the sake of doing a kindness. For the good of your soul — which I think needs it more than the Madigans' ever did!"

VIII

In the resulting hush Dr. Osborne wore the stunned expression of a man whose mirror had shown him a stranger, and Madigan, giving it up as a bad job, started to go look for Arabella.

Miss Sibyl rose from the wicker chair. She said swiftly, "I take it as a compliment, Mr. Madigan, that you brought the girl here to us. We accept our — ah — common duty! We are well able to do so."

Vastly relieved, Madigan inclined his head

in thanks to her.

"However," she pursued, "my brother is entitled to impose reasonable conditions." She met her brother's stare. "Allow me to modify them, Edward. We will give the girl a good home, Mr. Madigan, providing that you agree to remain in this locality in case the arrangement proves impractical. We will never turn her out, but it may happen that you will have to share with us the responsibility of making other arrangements for her. Does that seem fair to you?"

"I didn't come back to stay," he argued. "I don't fit into this part of the country. I'm a traveling man."

"I'm afraid you will have to suspend your travels for awhile, if you care for the girl's future welfare."

"How long?"

She hesitated, her old eyes searching his face. "Two years. Perhaps by the end of that time you will have made a place for yourself and settled down. Stability gives contentment. A man who finds no satisfaction in himself seeks for it in vain elsewhere. You may find difficulty in changing your habits, but you are still quite young enough to make the effort — for the good of *your* soul, Mr. Madigan!"

He smiled at her artful gibe. She was

cleverer than her brother. "So I've got to promise I'll stick around in call for the next two years, eh? It's a long time!"

He could promise easily, with a free conscience, and know that it wouldn't be broken by any act of his. The two lawmen waiting outside for him would do the breaking. Among the Sanburn townsfolk and all the surrounding ranchers, he couldn't think of one who might welcome him back. Nobody out there wanted a Madigan for neighbor, and the law waited to say so.

"I am sure you would keep your word," said Miss Sibyl.

Arabella came dashing into the parlor, tripping on her unaccustomed long skirt, tearing the gold-embroidered hem. She must have overheard the end of the conversation, for she shrilled at Madigan as she rushed to him, "Y'gotta stick round, Jim — y'gotta! I ain't gonna stay here 'thout you promise to — Aw, this goddam skirt!"

Miss Sibyl flinched.

"I'm giving my promise, Arabella," Madigan said, getting her quieted down. A twinge of conscience then stabbed him, and he carefully reframed his statement: "I promise to do everything I can to stay in these parts." A man couldn't swear to do more than his best.

"Solemn promise?"

"My solemn promise."

Arabella accompanied him to the front door, clinging to his arm, timid as if he were leaving her in a prison. Her eyes mutely implored him to take her away with him, and in compassion he stooped and kissed her. The Osbornes, following behind them, exchanged raised glances.

"You'll be learning so much here, the time will fly past, Arabella," he said, trying to cheer her. "It'll be strange to you at first, and maybe some of it won't be easy, but you'll learn pretty quick." And, he thought, you'll forget much of what is past, as you've already half-forgotten poor Jay. "Just be a good girl, and you'll do fine."

"Ain't I a good girl?" Her meaning was different from his.

"Sure you are." How much she had to learn!

It struck him that she was ending forever the only life she had known. The ways of the rawhiders lay behind her. She was standing tiptoe on the threshold of a new life that was strange and frightening.

He said with force, "Sure you're a good girl! Everything will be all right, honey, don't you worry!"

She smiled radiantly. "Ah ain't worryin' a

speck, Jim Madigan," she cried, "jest so you call me 'honey' — 'cause now Ah know you'll be a-comin' back to me!"

Lord, he thought; Lord help us. An unthinking word of affection, and she in her earthy innocence takes it as a token of betrothal, no less.

He gently freed her clinging hands from his arm, opened the front door, and walked out to the town marshal and the county sheriff — two grimly waiting men who, remembering only too well the troublesome years of the Madigans, firmly believed in stamping out a spark before it fanned up into wildfire.

Marshal Hilliard and Sheriff Calhoun were two of a kind, professionally, in that they both held office by catering strictly to the wishes of the leading citizens. It was expected of them, and they made no bones about it.

Sanburn had gone through its curly wolf days. When the turning point had come, it had been a complete about-face. Extreme looseness had spawned extreme tightness. The foremost merchants had formed themselves into a committee, passed a resolution to tighten up the town, and hired Hilliard to do it with the aid of a picked squad of helpers.

A tight town was what they had got, a town run by and for business. And there the pendulum had stuck fast. Hilliard's helpers were gone now; he didn't need them. In any dispute, the merchant was right and could call on Hilliard to back him.

The biggest ranchers of the county, members of the county cattlemen's association, looked to Calhoun to guard their special interests. They got him returned to office when election came around, and he served them faithfully, on the plain principle that those who supported him were men of worth; those who didn't were worthless.

If, in the execution of his duties, Sheriff Calhoun, like Marshall Hilliard, mangled the letter of the law, his supporters shrugged it off. The end justified the means, all agreed. A cattle country existed for cattlemen, and big cattlemen could do no wrong. Keep it that way.

Up and down the valley around Sanburn there were many small ranchers who didn't rate much standing. But they hoped to grow big some day and enjoy the privileges, so they struggled on hopefully and didn't kick hard against the order of things.

Marshal Hilliard spoke first, planting himself forward in Madigan's path and bluntly inquiring, "You moving on?" His girth had spread since Madigan had last seen him, and he had heavy jowls, but he retained his domineering manner as an efficient town tamer.

"Soon as I can pick up a dab of supplies," Madigan told him, "I'll be heading out of your bailiwick, don't worry." He'd had a slight run-in with him once. His older brothers had taken it up and set a hilarious deadfall for Hilliard, using a trip-wire and a bucket of whitewash.

"And out of mine!" Sheriff Calhoun commanded. "As soon as you can make it!"

This was predictable. While they waited outside for him, he thought he had prepared himself to meet them and accept without argument their notice to move on. He hadn't any inclination to stay, none whatever. The breaking of his solemn promise was on their hands.

It was their attitude that rubbed him the wrong way. Coming after his anger at Dr. Osborne, their attempt to bully him coiled his temper.

"I'm not so sure of that, Sheriff!" he said.

"Be sure!" Calhoun snapped. "When you got run out of this county, it meant don't come back!"

"That's a lie. I left of my own free will."

"Just in time, Madigan — only just in

time! I was about to come and prod you on your way!" Calhoun was getting along in years, and quick to resent disrespect, while at the same time he practiced a set of habits intended to disguise his advancing age: walked too fast, rode too straight-backed, spoke with a conscious voice of iron.

"Nobody ran me out," Madigan said. "No lawman breathed down my neck when I sold off the cows and horses, and left the ranch."

"Ranch!" Calhoun echoed. "That shack was nothing but a hangout on a piece of open range. Nobody's ever bothered to use it since the roof fell in."

"Maybe I'll fix it up for myself."

"Don't try! You can't buck me!"

On the verge of defying the sheriff, Madigan shrugged and turned to the two horses, his and Jay's. He had gone as far with defiance as he wanted to go. To let anger push it further would be not only reckless but against his own wishes. The sheriff was unknowingly doing him a favor by ordering him to move on out of the county.

Calhoun's iron voice brought Dr. Osborne out of his house. Arabella would have darted out, too, but Miss Sibyl drew her back and shut the front door. Ladies must positively never be seen in the vicinity of a public dispute: Arabella's first lesson.

"What's going on here in front of my house?" inquired the doctor, and his prestige was such that Marshal Hilliard touched his hat to him, bobbing his head in apology for the disturbance.

"Him!" Calhoun stuck a thumb at Madigan. "And he'll keep on going till he's clear out of the county, by my order!"

Dr. Osborne raised his eyebrows. "Indeed! Why? What has he done, for you to order him, ah, banished from your sphere of authority, might I ask?"

Calhoun blinked, first interpreting the question, then groping for a suitable reply, one that would reach the understanding of a gentleman whose knowledge of law enforcement was obviously limited.

"It's not what he's done, Doctor, so much as what he's likely to do! Raise hell, like him and his brothers did before, I mean, when they lived here. You remember. So I'm ordering him to get going."

"I see. A preventive measure. Admissible in medicine, but not, I believe, in law. You cannot legally impose a penalty upon a citizen because of what you may regard to be his possibly law-breaking potentialities. You cannot, in other words, arrest him for a crime before he has committed it."

"I can't?" It was a dangerously radical idea to the sheriff. He doubted its validity. "I've done it before!"

"Then you exceeded your authority and laid yourself open to lawsuit, Mr. Calhoun. However, that is not my concern. In this present case," Dr. Osborne went on crisply, "I *am* concerned."

"You doctoring Madigan for something?"

"No. I am concerned because he has given his word that he will not leave this locality for the next two years. He gave his word to me, to my sister, and to, ah, a young woman he brought to my house."

"Two years!" Calhoun exchanged a shocked stare with Hilliard. "I won't have it! He threatens he'll move back onto the old Madigan place."

"That hardly seems criminal."

"How would he make his living there? Rustling?"

They looked at Madigan — the doctor inquiringly, the two law officers skeptically. He shrugged and said with dry indifference, "Guess some of the outfits could use an extra roundup hand." He wished Dr. Osborne had stayed inside and let things run their straight course.

"The folks round here," remarked Calhoun, waxing heavily sarcastic, "are just panting to hire a Mad Madigan! It'd liven up the work and keep all hands happy! Look," he said with sudden earnestness, "don't you know how it is? It's not only your own rep — you carry the rep for your brothers, too! That's natural. Folks look at you, they remember everything the Madigans did."

"They remember the bad," Madigan agreed. "That's Sanburn for you."

"I knew the minute you hit town. So did Hilliard. All right, that's Sanburn, like it or not. Where've you been since you left? Hiring your gun out hither and yon, I bet!"

"Not often."

"Once is plenty! Gunhands and drifters ain't welcome here, not a bit. It's all changed. We've got a settled range, no problems, everything peaceful. Sanburn's the quietest, best-run town this side of the Pecos. Two years? I wouldn't give you two weeks!"

Dr. Osborne, with the bland assumption of a gentleman who had never had to scrabble for his beans, observed, "There must be some way for you to earn a living, Madigan. Didn't you and your brothers hunt wild cattle at times?" He had only a dim notion of what it implied, believing it to be a kind of sport, possibly invigorating if one cared for that sort of thing.

Madigan nodded. "Hunted the brush for mavericks and outlaw steers." He rolled his shoulders uneasily in recollection. The dizzying heat of the Brasada. The blinding dust and sweat. Snakes and centipedes and thick thornbush. The killing work.

"Well, you could do it again, couldn't you?"

"I guess so. If I had to," he admitted slowly, waiting for Calhoun's objections.

Marshal Hilliard, his grin humorless, made the remark that mavericking was first cousin to rustling, but Dr. Osborne said obliviously, "It's settled, then!" And he nodded with the satisfied air of having hoisted Madigan over the hump, by virtue of clear thinking.

"Not for me!" Calhoun objected. "He goes mavericking, next he's slinging a wide loop and a running iron! No offense meant, Doctor, but you just don't know!"

Dr. Osborne cast a cold look at him. "I know that you cannot restrict his right to free movement, nor deprive him of his means of livelihood, unless he has broken the law, Mr. Calhoun! That is tyranny, sir, and as a citizen I protest on principle! I invoke the Bill of Rights! Regardless of your misgivings, his future good conduct must be taken for granted."

The highflown language baffled Calhoun, and the reference to the Bill of Rights shook him, but he grasped the doctor's last sentence and reversed its edge.

"Do *you* take it for granted, Doctor? You took his word he'd stay. You're set against me running him out. All right!" He spread his legs, fists rammed on his hips. "Would you want to vouch for his good conduct the next two years? Tell me that!"

Dr. Osborne, taken aback by the direct challenge, opened his mouth, closed it, and glanced at his front door for inspiration. Having talked himself into a corner, he sought to avoid further involvement, without loss of dignity. To take a stand purely on principle was the mark of a superior man; getting down to earth was distasteful, especially if it entailed making a positive commitment. Madigan sincerely hoped he'd find a way out. A buckboard came bowling down the street, and the doctor was so pressed that he looked hopefully at it as a possible diversion to help him out of his dilemma. A patient, perhaps. An emergency case.

Calhoun smiled. "Well, Doctor, would you?" he asked, daring a hint of a jeer. Confident that he was on safe ground, he offered, "If so, I reckon he could stay. Yep, I'd let him stay on your personal whatcha-call-it — your recognizance." He smacked his lips over the word. By damn, he could sling the tall lingo, too.

Dr. Osborne again glanced toward his house. A lace curtain moved, falling back into its folds as a pale old face withdrew from the window. He said reluctantly, "Yes."

Calhoun hit his thigh a slap and muttered, "Damn!" He hadn't counted on Miss Sibyl. Neither had Madigan.

The oncoming buckboard drew over and halted before the house. Its team bore the H 7 brand, and from it sprang the H 7 range boss, wearing the badge of one of the county sheriff's sparetime deputies — Calhoun had them all around the county, all cowmen attached to the big outfits.

The range boss came stalking straight at Madigan, saying to Calhoun, "Get that sonofabitch! He shot Severne!"

Calhoun had a gun out instantly, trained on Madigan. "The hell! Henry Severne himself? But there he —"

"Got him in the arm. Right up at the house!"

"Doctor, there goes your vouch and his two years!" said Calhoun, openly pleased.

"He's already broken the law!"

The range boss caught hold of the front of Madigan's shirt. He was a hawk-nosed Texan in cold wrath, and he drew back his fist to smash Madigan full in his face. Calhoun kept his gun leveled, making no move to interfere, while Hilliard looked on interestedly. Anybody taking a shot at a big man like Severne could expect to get worked over.

It was Henry Severne, climbing down from the buckboard, a makeshift bandage on his arm, who said, "Lay off, Shade — lay off him!"

He ranged a look over the group, his expression not changing as he met Madigan's eyes, and spoke to Dr. Osborne.

"Drove in for you to patch up this arm, Doctor. Bullet went through. Scraped the bone, I guess. Hurts some."

At once professional, Dr. Osborne motioned him to go into the house. He sent Madigan a look of bitter exasperation.

Calhoun pushed at Madigan. "Get a move on!"

Henry Severne, starting toward the house, paused and turned. "Where-to you taking that pilgrim, Sheriff?" he asked.

"Jail!" Calhoun sounded surprised at the question.

"What's he done?"

"Mr. Severne! He ain't getting away with shooting you!"

Henry Severne stared steadily at Madigan. "Wrong man!"

"But Shade said —"

"Shade made a mistake. Got excited." The range boss looked as incapable of excitement as a frozen corpse. Henry Severne's eyes held Madigan's, silently sending the message: *Keep your mouth shut, and so will I!* "Right, Shade?"

Shade said tonelessly, "Right," catching the message and then laying a wicked stare at Madigan. "A mistake."

"Let him go, Sheriff!"

Entirely unconvinced, but automatically serving the will of a cattleman who was one of his most powerful supporters, Calhoun holstered his gun. "Dammit, Mr. Severne," he complained, "I needed to hang something on him! It'd put him out of the way. He's a Madigan — a trouble-maker born."

Severne's eyes stayed fixed on Madigan. "What was it I heard you say about 'his two years,' Sheriff?"

"He aims to stay that long. Gave his word to Dr. Osborne. It's got something to do with a young woman he brought here, far's I make out."

"A young woman?" Severne swung his head and inquired politely, "In your house, Doctor?"

Dr. Osborne's severe face stiffened. Disliking personal questions of any kind, he replied shortly, "My sister has taken her in. It is a private matter."

"Beg your pardon."

Watching Severne, Madigan saw his comprehension and his swift shuffling of facts and consequences. If Arabella was now under the wing of the highly respected Osbornes, less than before could Severne risk having it known that he had tried to force her to live with him. This was Texas. Big as he was, he couldn't afford the scandal and the general condemnation that was certain to follow. Everybody would turn against him. Facts would be garbled by gossip, until in all eyes he stood as a monster who had attempted to rape the Osbornes' fair and innocent young ward. Men had been mobbed and strung up for less.

"Mr. Severne," Calhoun urged, "don't you want to lay a charge against Madigan? Why not? You and Shade know it was him shot you! Shade don't make mistakes."

"I'm sure," Severne said. "Yeah, he did it, but it was an accident." He returned his stare to Madigan. "Let bygones be bygones, eh?"

"Suits me."

"*Bueno!* We understand each other. Guess we'll meet again, you stick around. By the way, we had a burial on H 7 last night. Right nice, under the trees."

"Who died?" Calhoun asked.

"Nobody you know. All right, Doctor, I'm coming."

Calhoun watched Severne enter the doctor's house, and after the front door closed he said sourly to Madigan, "I can't figure why he let you off. You don't deserve it a damn bit, pulling your gun on a charitable man like him. I'll be keeping my eye on you. One step out of line, you'll be where you belong!"

"Any time you come in town," put in Marshal Hilliard, "step light, Madigan — step awful light!"

Shade stroked his hawk nose with a forefinger. "Gentlemen," he drawled, "somethin' tells me he won't make the grade!"

Madigan gathered up the reins of the two horses. "Get off my back, all of you!" he said wearily, and went on down the street to trade Jay's saddle for some supplies to take out to the shack.

It was going to be a tough two years out

there. That shack was a hell of a *querencia.*

IX

In moments of meditation, Madigan concurred with the old axiom that time was man's most precious possession. Money spent could be earned again, health could be restored, but time gone was gone forever.

Walking down the main street with Arabella, he felt as if he had wasted a hundred years.

A stray blast of spring wind, fresh off the mountains, swept up dust. It had been a dry winter, a lean winter for him, the wild cattle drifting off to distant parts in search of water. Before the wind had passed on, doors and windows slammed shut all over town. He shook his high, dark head at the sound, at the thought of shutting out a fresh wind because of a bit of dust.

"That's Sanburn!" he commented. "Everything must come tidy, even a breeze. If they could, they'd damn nature itself to hell for not following their rules!"

"Jim!" said Arabella in a tone he had learned to know and recognize. Along with a look, it conveyed disapproval — the same look that he met in the eyes of Sanburn

111

folks. "Your language!"

He marveled once more at Miss Sibyl's success at taking an ignorant rawhider girl and shaping her into her own image. Miss Sibyl had died in her sleep, the tailend of the past winter, but she had left behind what amounted to a younger incarnation of herself.

Arabella had proved to be an apt pupil, quick to learn all that was taught her, and Miss Sibyl discovered in her a natural gift for mimickry which she developed and perfected to best advantage. Not only in her stilted speech and elegant mannerisms, but in her whole attitude she mirrored Miss Sybil. The same viewpoint, the same standard of values.

She had locked the door on her past life, shed herself of everything pertaining to it, and taken on an entirely different personality. What Madigan had first thought were conscious posings and affectations he came to realize were actually unconscious demonstrations of her ability to adapt herself completely to her environment.

She even critized his shabby appearance.

"You might have worn better clothes to come to town in!"

"I didn't ride thirty miles to cut a figure," he said. "I'm hoping to catch a job on one

112

of the spring roundup crews."

"Better appearance," she pronounced carefully, "might improve your prospects." Exactly as Miss Sibyl would have said it.

He smothered a grin, wondering if she ever recalled the morning he made her wash herself in a water hole and throw away her soiled cotton dress. It wasn't easy to connect that earthy waif with this immaculate person pacing with daintily little steps beside him. She moved with an air of smooth composure, blond and erect, not allowing a hint of emotion to mar the picture of a properly decorous young lady.

"These clothes I'm wearing are the best I've got. They'll have to do till I get some money." He glanced down at her hands; they were clean and soft, held primly folded as Miss Sibyl had instructed her to hold them when in public. "Do you find it hard, keeping house for the doctor?"

"I manage the house," she corrected him. "Two hired women do the housework."

"That should be a help."

He remembered her speechless awe upon first entering the Osborne home, her abysmal ignorance of household tasks, of decent cooking, and her sketchy notions of cleanliness. Now she ran the house and bossed the hired help. Probably did a good job of it.

The doctor seemed satisfied.

She had come a long way in a fairly short time. She had bridged a vast gap and made a respected place for herself.

No, those Trubbidge rawhiders hadn't gone all to seed. There was sound stock in them, needing the right push of fate for it to spring up and thrive. Under Miss Sibyl's guiding influence, Arabella had altered her family name to Truebridge. Maybe that was what it had been in the distant past, or something like it.

She could write it in a legible hand: *Miss Arabella Truebridge.* That was about as much literacy as a young lady needed for reasonable purposes, but she had gone on and soaked up more. She could make a stab at reading *The Beauchamp Manual Of Social Forms.*

Miss Arabella Truebridge, ward of Dr. Edward Kendall Osborne, who had considered his guardianship of her his bounden duty since his sister had died. There was some rumor that the doctor would legally adopt her as his daughter, for the sake of propriety. In his reserved way he seemed to have grown fond of her. Or perhaps he had become dependent upon her to make his home comfortable, and for that reason he concerned himself with her welfare.

She hasn't wasted her time here, Madigan mused, *as I've wasted mine.*

The folks here hadn't forgotten that he was a Madigan and therefore an unpredictable quantity, an alien. Nor would their eyes let him forget — as if he ever could — that he was different from them. He hadn't gained anything by staying on. There was the challenge of making a go of it and proving that he could keep out of trouble, but that wouldn't have held him if he hadn't given his word to stay.

He didn't often get to town. Living alone, he found that the crowd this Saturday filled a restless need in him, although nobody threw him a friendly greeting. The spring work was beginning. Ranchers were in to buy supplies and pick up extra hands, and cowpunchers had ridden in for a quiet whirl before roundup.

Marshal Hilliard, trotting by on horseback, touched his hat to Arabella and hauled in to ask Madigan, "How long since you seen Sheriff Calhoun?"

By its brusque form and tone, the question could have been aimed at a convict out on parole. "A few days back," Madigan answered. "He drops in on me every so often."

"Don't take it personal." Hilliard gazed at

several men listening along the boardwalk. "It so happens some folks are complaining of short calf-crops since you went to mavericking."

"So Calhoun's told me, more than once."

"Just a coincidence, I guess." Hilliard's tone verged on irony. "D'you happen to be acquainted with the rawhiders who're camped up the Pecos?"

Madigan glanced aside at Arabella. "What name?"

"You ought to get to town more often, Madigan. Keep up with things going on. They been camped around there a year or more. Some folks figure that's where their missing calves go, maybe with the help of a local man who knows the outfits, when and where to strike 'em, and all the ins and outs of this country. See what I mean, Madigan?"

"He sees!" somebody said, and Hilliard nodded.

"Romedy, they call themselves. A bad bunch. Shot up three fellers last winter, but Calhoun can't prove it. Didn't he tell you?"

Madigan shook his head. Arabella was walking on alone, obeying the precept that a lady must detach herself from any public discussion among males. "Calhoun only speaks to me about cows, and then not much. I've got no neighbors out there, and

I don't visit around when I come to town."

"Hm! Thought maybe you knew the Romedys — maybe on visiting terms with 'em. Well, I'm on my way to visit a fool who figures to light out without paying his bills." The marshal performed services of the kind for Sanburn storekeepers. He lifted his reins. "It won't take me long," he promised, meaning: *Watch your step in town while I'm gone!*

Containing his temper, Madigan paced on past the men along the boardwalk, feeling their silent antagonism. Hilliard's broad hints had helped toward solidifying their suspicions of him. They were losing calves, and in their eyes he was by logic the likeliest culprit. It didn't weigh much that Sheriff Calhoun's repeated inspections of his lonely little outfit had uncovered nothing against him. He was a mavericker who kept to himself, clouded by the stormy Madigan reputation. The logic ended there.

Arabella had stopped in front of Price's Emporium to speak with Dr. Osborne and Henry Severne. The doctor sat in his halted buggy, Severne standing beside it, smiling, a fine white Stetson held grandly on his arm in polite deference to the girl. Severne had kept to his bygones-be-bygones pact, and he nodded amiably to Madigan as he came up. Like Arabella, he apparently had wiped the past from his mind.

"What brings you out this time of day?" Dr. Osborne asked Arabella. He barely favored Madigan with a curt nod, having retained all of his intolerance and peppered it with prejudice gained from ugly rumors.

She made a small gesture toward the Emporium. "Mr. Price has the pair of shoes I ordered."

Henry Severne's bountiful supply of middle-aged gallantry surged to the fore. "The smallest shoes in the county, I wager!" he declared. "Your pardon, Miss Arabella," he poured it on expansively, "but in a fortunate moment or two my eyes had the privilege to inform me that your tiny feet are every bit as dainty as the rest of you!"

Arabella lowered her gaze modestly, murmuring, "Thank you, Mr. Severne."

"Ah, a gladsome sight you are! Eh, Madigan? Eh? What's the matter, man, can't you shape out a compliment to the belle of the county?" He nudged Madigan, heavily playful. "You think you're the lucky dog, but I'll cut you out yet, by dad, see if I don't!"

Madigan returned his grin. Odd; he had shot Severne and robbed him of his prey, yet now this was the only man who showed him any friendliness. "I wouldn't put it past

118

you to try," he allowed, remembering him at the Trubbidge camp and later.

"Hah! Listen to him!" Severne reared his head back. His deep laugh drew glances. "While you stick yourself out there in that lil' ol' poverty outfit, I'm right here making time!" He was an amazing mixture of ruthless brute, florid flatterer, and jovial hail-fellow-well-met.

Dropping his banter, he turned and said soberly, "That was a fine dinner at your house, Doctor. It truly honored and pleasured me. Miss Arabella's a credit to your dear departed sister, God rest her soul." And that was another side to him.

Slightly embarrassed, Dr. Osborne murmured that the pleasure had been his. He seemed somewhat overwhelmed by the rancher's large and vigorous personality, yet intrigued. Gathering up his lines, he said to Arabella, "You will be home shortly, then, I take it."

"Yes, Doctor, in a few minutes."

He drove on sedately to his house, his old horse as gravely dignified as himself.

Severne bowed to Arabella. "May the best man win!" he said to Madigan, and took himself off, donning his white Stetson with a flourish.

Madigan frowned after him. "Was he joking, or has he actually got the gall to try courting you?" he asked Arabella.

She lightly twitched her shoulders. "He comes to the house sometimes. He owns an interest in the bank, and he and the doctor talk about mortgages and things. We had him to dinner last week."

"Well, well — how we do change!"

"Mr. Severne is — is quite changed. His manner toward me is at all times most respectful." It was one of her precise sentences borrowed from Miss Sibyl. "And — and friendly," she added, less precisely.

"Friendly!" Madigan echoed. "He's old enough to be your father, but not old enough to shed his tomcat prowling! Bear in mind what he tried to make you into!"

"Please! Such things are not spoken of by people of good manners."

That — from a Trubbidge. He smiled to himself. "Maybe not, but that doesn't bury them. Go ahead and get your new shoes."

"Aren't you coming in with me?"

"No, I'll wait out here for you. Waiting around is the best thing I do these days." The restless craving to move on, to escape, came alive in his face, giving him suddenly a look that brought a startled stare from Arabella.

"Jim, you're so strange!"

"Strange?" He let his inner smile emerge. "That's what I think about you. About you and the rest of —"

He checked himself, knowing he was doing no good. Anything he said and did out of common was weighed, analyzed, probed for its worst meaning. Even Arabella had caught the habit, probably from Dr. Osborne who had heard the rumors and learned why mavericking was regarded as close kin to rustling.

"Go get your shoes," he told her again, and she went into the Emporium.

Waiting, the fancy came to him that his dead and gone brothers were wagging ghostly heads in disgust at the sight of the last of their firebrand brood, broke and friendless, hating his barren life here, but trapped by a promise. They wouldn't have promised, knowing blamed well they couldn't keep it and keep their sanity too. The shack had been little more than a headquarters to return to from time to time.

He shouldn't have promised. It was killing him. Cut loose, they would have said. To hell with it. You only live once, and life is short. It was short for us, but we sure crammed a lot into it.

X

He grew aware of someone talking in the penetrating drawl of a man who was intent upon making himself heard. A half silence had fallen, men in the street listening to the voice.

"Ev'rybody knows what rawhiders are! Sneak thieves! Calf snatchers! I don't have to tell you what else!"

The speaker rocked on spurred heels outside of the Sanburn Hotel & Bar, a group of H 7 hands grinning behind him and winking at one another. He looked a little drunk.

"Rawhiders," he proclaimed, "ain't got hardly no human morals at all! They mate up like houn' dawgs. We oughta go an' burn 'em out!"

Shade stepped out from the hotel, his lips curved down thinly beneath the hawk nose. "Snub that kind of talk, Holgast!" he snapped. "We don't burn anybody out, hear?"

The man he called Holgast flapped a hand at him. "You're boss on H 7 but off H 7 range I air my mouth! I'm roastin' the rawhiders." He cocked a look at Focht's General Merchandise Store, and raised his voice

122

louder. "Only diff'rence among rawhiders, some's worse'n others. Like the Romedy trash. The men rustle calves, an' the women —"

"You're a liar!"

The three short words were not loud, but they were clear and they cut across Holgast's voice. A slim figure walked from the semi-darkness of the store, going to a saddled horse and two pack horses at the hitching rack. The pack horses were loaded, ready to go, their burdens expertly roped on.

Holgast wheeled half around, feigning elaborate surprise. "Say, now, here's a Romedy in person! Speak of the devil. What was that you said?"

"I said you're a liar." The voice contained a slight huskiness, as Madigan keenly remembered it had.

"How awful!" Arabella whispered at Madigan's back. She held the wrapped shoes. "Imagine brawling with men in the street!"

"It's Dare Romedy."

"I know her. I mean, I once knew her. She —"

He shut his ears to her. He was gazing at Dare Romedy, remembering the softness of her black hair in his hands, her warm

123

chuckle, the hint of mockery in her emerald eyes.

She wore a man's sun-bleached sombrero and washed-out Levi denims that did nothing whatever toward hiding her femaleness. Moving on between the pair of pack horses, she gave a tug to the diamond hitches, a final test. She had said what she had to say, and now, unhurried and casual, she would be on her way, taking back supplies to her people.

Holgast left the H 7 group and advanced on her, and Shade shrugged and stood looking on with the rest. The threat of burning out the Romedy camp was evidently all that Shade objected to. He wasn't going to deprive Holgast of his sport with the girl.

Madigan also walked toward her. He knew what was coming. Holgast had baited Dare Remedy for the hell of it, setting a trap to devil her. That she had met it and told him off wasn't any surprise. She possessed a manlike courage, a courage that was liable to bring her to grief. As Holgast approached her, she stepped out from between the pack horses to confront him, rather than try springing onto her saddled horse and taking a hasty departure.

Madigan couldn't see her face; her back was toward him. He watched her hands, one holding a light quirt of braided leather with a broken wrist-loop, the other dipping into a pocket of her faded Levis. More clearly he foresaw what was all too likely to come of Holgast's baiting. He hoped it wouldn't, hoped something would nip it off in time.

Holgast stopped before her. "That's mighty strong talk from a lady!" he said, running a stare over her. His grin didn't reach to his eyes. "I mean it *would* be, if it was from a lady. Comin' from a trashy rawhider wench —"

He got no further along that scurrilous line. The leather quirt whistled smartly. Somebody began a laugh at Holgast's flinch and back-step, and swallowed it. The quirt left a livid streak across his mouth and wiped away his grin.

Up and down the street men looked on, their expressions varying between disapproval and entertainment. Nobody showed any intention of raising a protest, much less of interfering. To buck against cowmen — H 7 men at that — on behalf of a rawhider girl, an outcast, took a hardier fool than Sanburn could produce. The traditional code didn't stretch that far, here in Sanburn.

"Jim! Come back!" Arabella whispered after Madigan. "She brought it on herself!"

It was Shade who, seeing that the baiting had passed far beyond a joke, circled swiftly around the hitching rack. Holgast lunged at the girl, his arms hooked low for a crushing bearhug. Her left hand started upward from her pocket. The sun flashed on blued steel.

Shade swooped down on her from behind and grabbed her hand holding the pistol. He twisted her wrist and shook the pistol from her, and wrapped a long arm around her neck.

"No, you don't, girlie!"

She instantly kicked twice, once back-heel, once forward with her toe. Shade sucked a hissing breath and hopped off on one foot, clasping his shin, letting go of her.

"Goddam she-wolf!" Holgast snatched the quirt and tore it from her. He rubbed his kicked knee briefly and straightened up, flicking the quirt in her face. "I'll send you howlin' back to your scalawag tribe with marks to show 'em! A damn good taste o' this'll teach —"

"Holgast."

Madigan spoke the name evenly, but his tone brought stares to him. He stood midway in the street, his face darkly alight yet controlled, in his mind the certain knowledge that he was setting a stone rolling that would start an avalanche back on him.

Behind him he heard again Arabella's whisper: "Jim! Stay out of it!" That same note of criticism that he had come to know, sharper now, much sharper. She saw him as getting himself embroiled in a street brawl. She feared that some shadow of the disgrace might touch her.

And the nasal twang of Mr. Focht, owner of the general merchandise store, a leader of the merchants' committee, and the town's unofficial mayor: "I knew it! I knew it had to come some day! Where's Hilliard? Somebody go —"

"You want something?" Holgast asked. He searched Madigan's face. Shade muttered a word to him, and he tensed and grunted, "The hell!"

"Yes," Madigan said. "I want you to drop that quirt."

A storm was roiling in him. He wouldn't allow it to shake his disciplined calm, but it showed in his eyes, making them appear larger, black under the shading brim of his hat. He was suddenly all Madigan, a wild spirit within him casting off the shackles and whooping its freedom.

Watching faces turned somberly expectant. As plain as speech, their expressions said that an event had come that Sanburn had awaited — Madigan was about to cut loose and break the peace. Worse, he was picking a fight over a woman, a Romedy rawhider woman of no account. Must be something between them.

Holgast turned his body squarely to Madigan. Across the dozen yards of street they studied each other, while deepening silence settled about them.

"I'll drop this quirt right where it belongs! On her mouth first!"

"Don't do that," Madigan said, and he made it more of a request than a command, a truant shred of caution warning him to leave room for compromise.

The change in Holgast, from alert aggression to scorn, showed he misread the reason for the mild inflection. "Hear that, Shade? You're wrong about him!" He touched the red welt on his mouth. "He's folded! He's askin' me —"

"I asked. Now I'm telling you." The shred of caution fled. Madigan spoke three more words and put into them a bite that drove out any chance of compromise: "Drop that quirt!"

Holgast, jarred by the abrupt shift, inspected him intently. "Okay," he said.

Slowly, he lowered the upraised quirt. Dare Romedy moved a step aside from him, watching his face. Her action reminded Madigan of Arabella — that other Arabella who had stepped aside and exposed Henry Severne to a bullet. Holgast opened his fingers wide, letting the quirt fall. Before it touched the ground, his spread hand sliced to his holster.

Madigan's fingers plucked the gun from his hip. Clean and smooth, he swung the gun up and fired a single shot.

It was an uncommon kind of draw, made with the minimum of motion. The movement of his arm didn't reach to his shoulder. His elbow was the swivel point, and he pitched the shot with the action of tossing a ball underhand, with a swift flick of the wrist. His emergency draw.

A second shot, tardier than an echo, exploded, Holgast's cocked gun striking the ground and going off. The bullet skimmed dirt and whirred down the street to smack into a side wall of the barbershop, bringing forth the startled barber and a lathered customer.

Holgast bent his head and regarded his right arm. Its shirtsleeve was taking on a dark stain, and blood began trickling down his hand. He raised his eyes, looked at Madigan, and down again — not at his arm, but at his fallen gun.

"Leave it," Madigan said. "I don't need to

kill you. I've never yet had to kill a man."

He felt the condemnation of all onlookers. Townsmen were staring at him as if he had made an arrogant brag after shooting a man for no real cause. Cowmen's eyes bitterly resented his having bested a cowman. The H 7 men looked at him stonily, waiting for Shade to make a move.

Shade picked up Holgast's gun. Madigan still had his gun out, and Shade said to him, "You're pretty fast, but I'd take you on."

"If you feel you've got to, go ahead," Madigan told him.

"Not here. Town won't stand for it."

"Name the time and place."

Henry Severne called from an open window of the hotel, "No more of that! Shade, get Holgast to the doctor. Rest of you get on back to the ranch."

They obeyed him. Severne was reputed to pay the highest wages in the county, and he kept the full crew on the year around, not trimming down to a skeleton crew through winter as others did. Madigan watched the H 7 men troop to the livery yard for their horses, before turning his eyes in search of Dare Romedy.

She was coming toward him, and for the first time he had a full view of her face by daylight. He didn't know whether she was beautiful or not. The impression she gave was one of warm life and color, and of a controlled calm that matched his own. She didn't have the beauty of Arabella, but to compare them was to compare the dawn with candle-light.

"Thank you, Jim Madigan," she said, smiling. "This is twice we've met, and trouble for you both times. I seem to bring you bad luck."

As before with her, he straightway made known her effect upon him. "I'll take any bad luck you bring me," he said, "sooner than I'd take good luck from anyone else."

She didn't lower her eyes from his. "Perhaps it's Henry Severne. Perhaps he brings us both bad luck."

"Severne?" At the moment he had to wrench his racing thoughts off her to recall who Severne was. "Whatever brings us together is good."

"You're as direct as ever. As fast." She tucked a fold of her shirt into the waistband of her Levis. The parting of her lips drew Madigan's ready attention. He thought they were painted, then saw they were not; it was their contrast against the golden tan of her skin.

Mexican? No, she possessed the supple

figure and the easy grace that went with it, but he doubted if she had any Mexican blood. Those clear emerald eyes. The fine softness of her thick hair.

To tuck in her shirt she drew in her slim waist, which raised her breasts. She caught his downward look, strongly masculine, and she colored slightly but finished her small task. In the next instant his gaze locked with hers, and he said, "I'm glad I'm a man, and you're glad you're a woman. I remember we said that."

What his eyes were saying was: *Whatever you are, whoever you may belong to, I want you for mine!*

She lifted her head proudly. "We said that, yes. I haven't changed. Nor you."

Why, she was more than beautiful. The realization led him to move closer to her, guardingly. He had a hunger for beauty. "I must see you again! Soon!"

"Perhaps not soon. You took up for a Romedy." A hint of sadness crept into her eyes. "Nobody here does that."

"I'm not Sanburn folks. I'm a Madigan, from up north."

"I know. You don't belong here, any more than I do. They won't forgive you." Her understanding gaze went past him, to the onlookers, to the front of Price's Emporium.

132

"I'm afraid it has cost you more than it was worth. Goodbye — unless you want to go with me? To the Pecos? Now?"

He held himself in. "I'm a — a pauper."

"So?" Mockery tinged her voice. "As if that matters!"

"I gave my word I'd stay two years. My time's not up yet."

"I see." Her gaze returned to the front of Price's Emporium, where Arabella had retreated under the entrance. "I see," she repeated quietly. "Goodbye, Jim Madigan. . . ."

XI

His eyes followed her riding off up the main street leading the two pack horses. She rode a black horse, as she had the evening he had met her in the Trubbidge camp on Hunter Creek; a fine big horse having the lines of a blooded racer. Strangely splendid mount for a rawhider.

When she was gone from sight he still stood facing after her, until conscious that men were looking at him. He ran a glance over them and saw that their eyes were cynically knowing, charging him with secret connections with the Romedy rawhiders

133

and with more than passing acquaintance with Dare Romedy.

Dr. Osborne came stamping up to him. The sound of the two shots had brought him outside, and he had met Shade and Holgast making for his house and got from them their version of the fight. Before attending to his latest patient, he had a statement to make to Madigan. He made it short and excessively sharp.

"Don't ever come to my house again, nor speak to Arabella!"

"Is that what she wants, too?" Madigan asked him.

"It certainly is!"

"I'm free of my promise, then?"

"You are!"

"Thanks."

He wanted to laugh out loud. Here was his reward for a chunk out of his life. It had gone for nothing, all the scrabbling for beans, the loneliness, the maddening frustration of sticking to a godforsaken spot as the prisoner of his sworn word. A single misstep branded him as a troublemaking pariah.

The hell with it. He had nothing to reproach himself for. He had kept to his word until it was flung back into his face. He was released from his deadening responsibility

134

toward Arabella. Even Miss Sibyl would have granted that. Even Jay.

Walking to the livery yard for his horse, he sent a farewell look after Dr. Osborne. Arabella, clutching her parcel of new shoes from Price's Emporium, had joined the doctor hurrying to his house. She looked back at Madigan. She shook her head furtively and made a small, uncertain sign to him, a fluttering of fingers.

He slowed his fast stride. His eager sense of freedom faltered. Was she still leaning on him, reluctant to let him go, bidding him to stay? The doctor had spoken only for himself, then, and not actually for her. That was the meaning of her headshake and sign. Despite her self-assured airs, inside she was unsure; she was afraid to break off the last tie with her former life. She was holding him to his solemn promise, no matter what Dr. Osborne said to the contrary.

"Oh, Lord, no!" he breathed. "No!" But just before going into the house with the doctor she looked back once more at him. A confirming look, half demanding, half pleading.

He sighed, exasperated by her persistence. He would have to find an opportunity to talk to her and convince her how utterly impossible it was for him to stay on. She had to be made to realize that she must stand on her own feet, not on his sacrifice.

"Damn that promise!" he muttered, wishing to shrug it off and go his way.

The onlookers had drifted off, turning their backs on him. A coin clinked on the ground near him. He looked down at a silver dollar, then around to see who had thrown it and why. His eyes caught a movement at the open hotel window that Severne had called out from, and he made out Severne standing in the shadowed interior of the room.

Severne made a beckoning motion to him and held up three fingers: *Come to Room Three.*

Madigan nodded, picked up the dollar, and took it into the hotel. He guessed Severne didn't take kindly to the shooting of one of his men. That was all right, but let him not get too roaring tough about it.

"Holgast only got what was coming to him," said Henry Severne indifferently. "Forget it. He's a fool when he's had a few drinks." He set out a full bottle and two glasses on the table in the hotel room. "Lucky for him it's my rule never to fire a man."

Madigan poured half a glass for himself. "Never?"

"Never yet. It's better he's taught a lesson. He was trying to fly high. Too bad it had to be you who took him down. When are you leaving?"

Madigan guessed that the question was Severne's main reason for inviting him to the room. "Not right away," he replied, and watched for a reaction. "There's something I've got to tend to first."

"Is it worth jail? Hilliard, soon's he gets back —"

"He won't find me in town."

"How about Calhoun? He covers the whole county. He'll hunt for you."

"I'll keep out of his way," Madigan said, deliberately terse. No doubt Severne wanted rid of him, a man who possessed first-hand knowledge of a shameful episode in his life.

Concernedly, Severne shook his head. "You can't hide out long before somebody turns you in. Calhoun's got deputies plastered all over the county. And you're no-ways popular, y'know, 'specially with these little outfits — they're the ones who're losing calves. I feel morally certain you're no thief. Not your style. But —"

"Thanks."

"But the little fellers don't share my opinion. They're bad off. They've got to blame somebody. You're it, you and the

Romedys. They think you're likely hand-in-glove together on the steal, with you the spotter."

"You paint it pretty black," Madigan observed. "Just how bad off are they? I haven't been keeping up with things."

"They're coming up damn short on their calf crops this spring," Severne told him. "It'll cripple 'em, come time to meet their notes at the bank. Then there's this drought. They don't suffer from that directly, no — they've got deep springs to fall back on. But some of the big fellers are naturally crowding 'em for water."

"You?"

Severne shrugged. "I'm one," he frankly admitted. "I'm not about to see my cows perish! Come a drought, you push for water any place you can get it — if you've got the men. I've got men, not nursemaids!"

"Like Holgast." Madigan let only a slight irony edge his tone. "Like Shade for ramrod."

"Sure! My crew's a tough bunch. Got to be. Mine's the nearest range to the Romedy camp, but I don't lose any calves. The Romedys know better. They steal from these little outfits that can't afford night guards. It's easier. Safer."

"Any doubt about that?"

"About it being the Romedys?" Severne looked surprised at the question. "None at all. I know it for a fact. That camp of theirs — well, picture it for yourself. It's on a low bank at a bend of the Pecos, couple miles east of what used to be a little Mexican village called Arruga."

"I know where you mean," Madigan said. "Passed by there once." Arruga's few inhabitants had died out or abandoned the village long ago.

Severne nodded. "The Romedy camp's got good grass down there on the riverbank. It's closed in by high bluffs on this side; only one trail down and they guard that day and night. Only other way to get to it is swim — and the Pecos runs deep and fast there at the bend. They've built a big log raft that they haul across with ropes. They never leave it on the other side."

"Maybe they like privacy," Madigan suggested, and Severne laughed, taking it as a joking remark.

"For good reason! They ease the stolen calves down their guarded trail, raft 'em over the river, and drive 'em on up into New Mexico to sell. Oh, I know their tricks!"

"Do they ever cross your range?"

"We've seen signs they do."

"You could put a stop to it easy enough,"

Madigan said, "if that's how they work it. Calhoun could have a dozen deputies waiting on the other side."

Severne smiled out into the sunlit street. "Why would I do that? They don't hurt me. It's the little outfits they're hurting. That suits me! I want this range around here. I need the deep springs for insurance against droughts. When these two-bit outfits go broke, the bank forecloses on their mortgages — and I control the bank!"

Madigan blinked at his brazen frankness. "Why are you telling me?" he asked, suddenly uneasy, distrustful. "That's a damn dangerous secret for me to know!"

Severne shook his head, still smiling. "It's no secret to Shade and the crew. They know what H 7 needs, to prosper through the dry years. It's safe with them, and it's safe with you. I like your style. Knew you'd kick the harness off sooner or later, and show the stuff in you." He pointed a finger at Madigan's glass. "You ain't touched your drink. When I invite a man like you to drink with me, it means something. You ought to know that."

"I do," Madigan said, "but I don't get the meaning."

"I'm offering to put you on my crew."

Madigan swallowed the drink and kept his

head tilted back, giving himself a moment to think. He said slowly, "Leaving out Hilliard and the sheriff, anybody hiring me now would stand to get blacklisted."

"No argument there!" Severne agreed. "So we keep it quiet till this blows over. Holgast won't throw any charge against you, I'll see to that. And I'll work on Calhoun to lay off." He refilled both glasses. "H 7 is your best hideout, and I pay good wages. Well? Do we drink to it?"

Leaning back in his chair, Madigan eyed him closely, seeking a reason for his own lingering distrust. "It sounds like an everlasting job, after what you've told me. I can see why you never fire a man! I don't like to tie myself down."

"You can draw your pay any time you want to quit. I'll give you a month's advance now, if you need it."

"You make me wonder if you've forgotten I shot you once!"

Severne flapped a hand impatiently. "I'm not one to hold a grudge. Let bygones be bygones, I said then, and I say it again. You've got guts and you don't talk much. You're the kind I want on H 7."

"Where you can keep your eye on me?"

"What d'you mean by that?"

"I was thinking of Arabella," Madigan

141

murmured.

He thought it would bring on an angry explosion that might expose hidden motives. Severne tightened his hands into fists, staring at him over the table, but at last he said ruefully, nodding at the window, "I saw her look back at you in the street. All right, dammit, I *am* mighty taken with her! I'd like to marry her!"

"Marry — her? Arabella?" Madigan came perilously close to a laugh. "You?"

Severne's big iron-gray head reared belligerently. "Why not? Think I'm too old for her, do you?"

"You'll admit there's some considerable difference in years!"

"Hell, the Severnes are long-lived! And we keep our manhood ripe a long time, let me tell you! I'm good for another thirty or forty years!"

"Could be," Madigan said. "It's the marrying part that surprises me. Do the women get more scarce at your age?"

Severne's eyes chilled, but again the outburst failed to materialize. "It's high time I started a family. A man gets to thinking, y'know, as years go by." He frowned, gazing broodingly into nothingness. "You get to thinking maybe you're not a full man till you're raising a few strapping sons to carry

142

on for you, and a daughter or two to take care of the house. You wonder if you're not missing out on something."

Here was yet another side to him, a thoroughly human yearning for family and a domestic life. The fact that his choice had fallen on Arabella, less than half his age, was probably a result of his lasting frustration over losing her. But at least his present intentions were aboveboard.

"Arabella would suit me for my wife. She's got a good build for child-bearing," he said, as if discussing the conformations of a likely young mare. "Of course, it's up to her," he added somewhat regretfully. "Can't make her marry me, like I did a German girl one time. Settler's daughter. Friend of mine, a gambler, played fake preacher. It didn't last."

"I shouldn't think it would've," Madigan said, wondering how many girls this bull of a man had ruined, one way or another.

"No, the doctor wouldn't stand for anything like that. It's Arabella's choice, not mine."

"Nor mine."

Severne nodded absently. "Let the best man win." He drew his faraway gaze back to Madigan. "By God, but I can offer her a hell-sight more'n you ever can! I'll have half the county in my hand before I'm through!"

"By breaking the little outfits!" Madigan snapped.

Severne grunted a curse, rising to his feet. "I'm not doing anything illegal. The Romedy's are doing it for me, and I'm not responsible for it, get that in your head!" He paused. "They've got a bunch of fine big horses they stole somewhere, that I wouldn't mind having," he said reflectively. "All blacks. But, hell, that can wait its turn. I'm not about to wreck the setup as she stands. Do I sign you on my crew?"

Madigan hesitated. He had to hole up somewhere out of Sheriff Calhoun's sight, until he could arrange a meeting with Arabella and convince her that it was best that he drop out of her life. His sense of responsibility toward her, and the memory of Jay, stubbornly refused to let him simply ride off. A couple of H 7 pay days, and he could be on his way with a small stake and a clear conscience.

"I'll try it. And thanks."

"Good!" Severne clapped him heartily on the shoulder. "Don't thank me. Glad to have you. Ride out of town like you're going out to your shack, then circle back and head to H 7. Play it safe, y'know. What folks don't know won't hurt anybody."

"Won't Shade and the hands talk?" Madigan asked, doubting his welcome on H 7.

For a bare instant cold humor glinted in Severne's eyes. "Not on your life, man — not on your life!" he vowed. "They know how to keep quiet. . . ."

XII

From somewhere above the gray mists of sleep there came a sound of urgency, and Madigan brought himself awake to meet it. Bunks creaked, men half rising, muttering. Somebody hissed for silence. Moonlight on the bunkhouse windows glimmered on faces that were set in the concentration of listening.

"What's wrong?" Madigan asked before he collected himself to remember where he was. Nobody answered him.

The lack of any reply cleared his head like a dash of cold water. He didn't repeat the question. Since the day he had arrived, not one of the H 7 hands had spoken to him except from necessity. A group of them could be casually talking, laughing, and at his approach they would close their faces.

They played no tricks on him, of the kind a new hand might expect: tricks to signify

145

that he was initiated and accepted, or rough-house tricks to test his temper. None of that here. They shut him out with a wall of sardonic politeness. Henry Severne had let them know that he had hired Madigan as a troubleshooter in case of need. Madigan didn't care much for the distinction, but it did afford him a few privileges. Shade never gave him a direct order, and he hadn't yet been called on to ride night guard.

Listening with the others, he placed the sound that had awakened them all. A horse was coming at a run, the furious drumming of its hoofs sending forward the message of emergency. Some of the men padded on bare feet to the bunkhouse door, and Madigan joined them. Lights came on in the rear windows of Severne's big house.

The rider pounded up to the front of the house and yelled for Severne, in his hurry ignoring or forgetting the rule that hired hands used only the rear, where the yard stretched bare and hard-packed between the house and the bunkhouse. The grass in front rarely suffered a hoofprint.

Severne answered him. The rider spoke briefly. Severne cursed. Their voices fell and couldn't be heard. Then Shade was calling out, "Get dressed, everybody, and saddle up! Madigan?"

"Right here!"

"Sounds like a job for you, troubleshooter! Jump to it!"

Severne appeared at the back door. "Never mind the others, Shade — just have 'em saddle up three horses. Make it fast! You and Madigan can handle this. And me. You ready?"

"Like always."

"Come here."

Three men stamped into their boots and ran to the corrals. Madigan pulled on his clothes and buckled his gun belt, while the rest of the crew idled back to their bunks. He felt their eyes coldly following him as he left the bunkhouse. They didn't like anything about him, the damyankee. He had got along with all kinds of people, including Texans — Jay, for one — but these secretive spooks had hatred in their souls. Holgast's downfall didn't set well with them, of course. And although Severne had over-looked *his* defeat, they evidently did not.

Severne and Shade were talking in low tones on the back porch, waiting for the horses to be brought up. In answer to Madigan's inquiring look, Severne said, "That was Redlinger who rode in. Seems to be a little mixup out there. Some of our fellers ran into a bunch of calves headed for the river, and got shot at."

"The Romedys?"

"Who else?" Severne had dropped the urgency that previously marked his tone. "Redlinger's gone back to tell the others we're coming. The Romedys can run stolen calves through my range, but damned if we stand for 'em to shoot at us!"

"Prob'ly mistook our fellers for deputies in the dark," Shade remarked.

"Mistake or not, that's going too far! Eh, Madigan?"

"It is."

"Glad you agree. Glad you don't let your friendship with that Romedy girl sway you in favor of her folks. Or do you?"

"I'm drawing H 7 pay," Madigan said curtly.

Severne nodded vigorously. "A man's first loyalty is to his outfit — right! I'll let you prove it to Shade. He's none too sure of you."

"All he's got to do," Shade drawled, "is show me."

The three hands brought up the saddled horses. They had gone to the trouble of catching Madigan's own horse for him and cinching on his own saddle. Madigan wouldn't have put it past them to provide him with a moon-wiping jughead calculated

148

to separate him from his backbone. He thanked the man leading it. The man replied that he figured a feller liked the feel of his own horse under him when and if he got into a tight scrape.

"Let's get out there before it's all over," Severne said, and they mounted and set off.

They rode in the course of the vanished Redlinger, up the long, rough slopes of the foothills, Shade leading the way with unerring knowledge of the terrain and an accurate comprehension of where the run-in had occurred. It seemed unlikely that they would find anything worth hurrying for by this time. Shade, though, suddenly threw up his hand for a halt. The blunt shadows of the higher hills lay ahead, the moon sinking behind them.

They listened to an oncoming rumble and a blatting of calves, punctuated by occasional gunshots. "Some kind of a running fight going on," Shade said matter-of-factly. "Coming from west. They'll swing down this side o' the hills. We hit it dead on the nose!"

"You did," Madigan said, giving him credit for a perfect sense of direction and timing.

"I know this range," Shade murmured modestly, and spoke to Severne. "Sounds to me like a lively scrap. Wish now you'd let me bring the crew. Could you cut on back for 'em?"

"Are you trying to protect me?" Severne demanded.

"There might be a killing. You don't want mixed in it. It's what you're paying Madigan for." Shade laid a flat look on Madigan. "If you're right about him, he don't even need me!"

Severne reined around. "All right, I leave it to you."

"You couldn't leave it in better hands!" Shade drawled, and dug spurs. "Let's head off that party, Madigan!"

Soon they could see the bunch of running, bawling calves, a patch of black ripples passing through the broad moon-shadows of the hills. Three riders bobbed up, bearing away from the calves, abandoning them. One was Redlinger, on a spent horse. He sent forward a hail:

"Shade? Goddammit, you cut it close! They —"

"Light for home — we'll take over!" Shade interrupted him. "Madigan, you get behind the calves, on this side. I'll circle round on the other side. We'll surprise those jiggers!"

"Any idea how many of 'em?"

"What d'you care, troubleshooter? You've

had it easy, an' now you earn your pay! Show me!"

Madigan heeled his horse forward and raced aslant of the calves, heading for their rear where the kicked-up dust obscured the pursuers. A fourth rider whirled across his path, another H 7 man, shouting something to him, pointing back and riding on.

It all had an unreal quality about it. He tried to piece the parts together, tried to detach his mind from haste. The H 7 hands were tough, as Henry Severne had bragged; tough in the cool, taciturn way of tough Texans. Yet four of them had turned tail and run, chased over their own range by calf-thieves. It said much for the Romedys, so dangerous that they stuck with their steal and rammed it through, regardless of H 7 opposition.

But then there was Shade, scorning the odds, ready to take on any number of Romedys with Madigan's help, while at the same time doubting Madigan's loyalty to the outfit. As range boss, the H 7 ramrod, Shade had to be tougher than the rest of the crew. It was that kind of outfit. And he was. But he wasn't reckless. He wasn't foolhardy, dashing in at unknown risks.

Madigan gave it up. There were few men whose reactions you could predict with certainty when the chips were down. Horsemen were coming, riding determinedly after the bunch of calves. He heard them, and glimpsed them advancing under the lee of the hills. A solid group. So many of them. He put their number at fifteen or twenty.

He reined in, setting his horse broadside, drawing his gun. Where was Shade? Did Shade imagine that the two of them could stand off that many Romedys?

A rifle cracked three fast-spaced shots. He didn't see the flashes; the shots came from behind him, from the spot where he had parted from Shade. His stiff-braced horse jerked, stood for an instant shivering, and collapsed under him.

He threw himself clear and got to his knees. "What the goddam hell!" he swore, then had to duck down low behind his dead horse. The oncoming group of horsemen were firing at him. They had seen the flurry of his fall in the dustladen shadow. They knew he was an enemy, for they rode close-packed together as a unit. A grim unit, fully prepared to shoot first at anything ahead.

He heard the impact of bullets striking his dead horse. He fired at the group, aiming high, hoping — a slim hope — to turn them back. They came on. How many Romedys were there? A family, a clan, a whole great tribe of them?

Somebody rapped a command. The gunfire slackened. The group split. They came at him from two sides, and a voice blared, "Lay down your gun, you sonofabitch — we gotcha!"

The familiar ring of the voice sent its shock — Madigan had heard it so often, Calhoun dropping in at his isolated shack, inspecting the lean gather of wild cattle and mavericks from the brush. Calhoun warning him, needlessly telling him to watch his step.

He called out, "Sheriff, lay off! This is me — Madigan!" He got half up from behind his dead horse, raising a hand.

Riders swarmed around him. He got an impression in the fading moonlight of Calhoun's face, of other faces as hard, of cold eyes over leveled guns, and he said, "Calhoun! Don't be a damn fool! I'm riding for Severne!"

An arm reached down and batted the gun from his hand, violently. He let it fall, thinking that Sheriff Calhoun wanted him for shooting Holgast, thinking that Severne would clear him of that charge. Severne came riding up the slope, to rein in among the group and stare down at him.

"Well, now!" Severne's voice was heavy;

the voice of a man admitting his fault. "I 'lowed he was a wild'n, but I said all along I didn't think he was a thief. So much for my judgment! Catch any of his pals, Calhoun?"

"Not a one," the sheriff answered disgustedly. "They quit him in the pinch. You know how slippery the Romedys are. We didn't even get a good look at 'em."

Madigan got to his feet, grasping the substance of Henry Severne's words. "Severne — !" he began. One of the sheriff's posse, a small rancher, rammed a forearm at his mouth.

"You'll get your chance to talk in court!"

"No call to bust his teeth in, is there?" Severne objected mildly.

"He's lucky he's alive!" the rancher retorted. "Some o' my calves are in that bunch!"

"All the same, I don't go for beating up a prisoner. I might mention you're on my range."

"Damn right we are!" another posseman put in. "And our calves are on your range!"

"Meaning what?"

Sheriff Calhoun asserted himself, saying, "Let's don't go making hints, just on the word of a thief! Mr. Severne, when we closed in on Madigan he tried to throw us off by claiming he was an H 7 hand. He yelled out he was riding for you."

"*Wha-a-at?*" Severne stared around at them. "He did? By God, that puts a different color on it!" He nudged his horse quickly on to Madigan. "You lying sonofa-bitch!" His right arm whipped over, gun in hand, and he struck downward.

Madigan didn't hear Sheriff Calhoun's half-hearted protest at having his prisoner buffaloed; nor Henry Severne's indignant comment that he hoped he had killed him . . . that he wasn't letting any damyankee cast a lie at him and the good name of H 7, ever.

Bright sunlight on his face wakened him. It poured in through a small window, hurting his eyes, and for relief he rolled his head away from it. Bare walls surrounded him, in one of them a strap-iron door. He forced his aching eyes to take another glance at the small, high-set window. Three vertical steel bars guarded it.

He sat up on the iron cot, holding his throbbing head, his feet feeling for the floor. Nobody had removed his boots, and he didn't have the ambition to tug them off. His head was bandaged, and he felt the roughness of dried blood on his face.

He heard himself say hoarsely, "I want a drink!"

A chair scraped. Marshal Hilliard presently loomed up at the strap-iron door, cigar in mouth. "Here y'are." He thrust a tin cup of water between the bars. "They gen'rally wake up asking first, 'Where am I?' Guess you're unusual. Or maybe you know."

Madigan stumbled to the door. Dizzy, he clung onto it. "The Sanburn jail." He got the tin cup to his lips and drank thirstily. "More!"

The cup rattled against the bars. "We aim to please."

Returning with the refilled cup, Hilliard said, "Well, Calhoun fin'ly laid you by the heels! Feel low?"

"My head!"

"You got it resisting arrest."

"I did?"

"That's what the charge sheet says. You'll soon get over it." Hilliard and all the cheerful unconcern of a disinterested spectator. "On the end of a high rope!" He chuckled at his own humor.

Dull apathy fogged Madigan's mind. "How soon?" he asked dully.

"Circuit judge is due this week. A man got killed last night, chasing after his calves. Maybe you didn't do it, but you're all we've

156

got. Nothing less than hanging will satisfy folks, so don't get any hopes up."

"It's all settled, then."

Hilliard nodded, taking back the emptied cup. "Why, sure. You know you're guilty. Ev'rybody knows it. Nobody's s'prised. We all knew your quiet ways since you came back was just an act." He ambled back to his office, whistling.

Madigan sat on the cot under the barred window and stared at the floor. After awhile he began to laugh, although it shot pains through his head. He was laughing at himself, the only one of the Madigan brothers who had tried to live a quiet and law-abiding life, the only one who would end his life on the end of a rope.

"Funny!" he mumbled. Weariness bent his head low. The floor heaved and the barred window began a slow, circling dance. He fell over onto the cot and relinquished his grip on his fading consciousness.

At some later hour Hilliard woke him up to ask him if he wanted to eat.

"The county's paying for it."

Madigan's stomach informed him that food was the last thing he could cope with this ghastly day, no matter who paid for it. He feebly waved it away.

"No sense wastin' it," Hilliard said.

"Guess I'll eat it m'self."

XIII

Somebody was unkindly pelting hard little objects at him. He raised a sheltering arm over his face, dragged upon his eyes, and found the cell dark. "What the hell?" he muttered.

One of the objects struck his arm and rolled onto the floor. He felt down for it, thinking vaguely of stones and of days long ago when, it was said, thieves had been stoned to death. His searching fingers encountered a small cylinder. He picked it up, his senses leaping at the familiar feel of it, knowing it to be a cartridge.

"S-s-ss-t!"

The cautioning hiss sounded from the high-set window above the cot. He looked up at it. Against the night sky its square outline showed a lump at the bottom. He saw the lump move. He climbed onto his feet and reached up, and touched fingers. The fingers pushed the lump into his hand and withdrew.

The gift was a gun, a Dragoon .44 by the feel of it, altered to take centerfire shells. He listened to a whisper of footsteps softly retreating. Mechanically, he broke open the gun. It was fully loaded. He knelt and searched over the cell floor for the objects that had struck him, and gathered a handful of spare shells.

The stooping sent fresh pains through his head. He stood upright, taking in the realization that he actually held a loaded gun in his hand. The question of who had provided it was relatively unimportant, though a mystery. There was no man he could call a friend, since Jay. Jay would have done it, certainly.

Sudden noise and a shaft of light sent him instinctively into a crouch. The light came from Marshal Hilliard's office lamp. The marshal was carrying it. He had been sitting outside in the street, talking with somebody, and keeping check on the town. Madigan shoved the gun under his shirt. He held his left arm over the bulge that it made.

Holgast and Shade came in with Hilliard. The summer work should have been keeping the range box occupied on H 7, so his presence in town had only one explanation: acting in his capacity as a deputy sheriff, he was here to make sure that Madigan didn't receive visitors or get any opportunity to give his version of the rustling operation.

The sight of Shade's hawk-nosed face brought facts suddenly clear to Madigan. He hadn't been in a condition to do much thinking. Now the pieces clicked together. Redlinger and the others, out stealing calves while supposedly on night guard, had got into a jackpot too big for them to handle.

And Severne made me the goat!

Severne had been holding him in reserve for just such an occasion, and the whole H 7 crew had known it. Hiring him on the quiet and keeping it secret, artfully taking him into his confidence, building him up as the troubleshooter. . . . "Let bygones by bygones." "I'm not one to hold a grudge." "May the best man win."

All of it a patient and deliberate frame-up calculated to kill him and pin the rustling onto him, removing any suspicion from H 7. Shade had seen to it that he rode his own horse last night, not an H 7 animal. Shade had shot his horse down and left him to Sheriff Calhoun's posse.

The only hitch was that the posse hadn't blasted him to rags because he called out to Calhoun, who reached him first. With all his faults, Calhoun wasn't a killing lawman of the coldblooded kind. Severne had tried with his gunbarrel to remedy that detail. It was up to Shade to round off the job, neatly

160

and lawfully.

Marshal Hilliard peered in through the bars of the cell door, holding his lamp up high. "Shade heard you moving around," he said. "What're you up to, standing there in the dark?"

"Stretching my legs," Madigan answered him. "They're stiff."

"Well, lay down!" Hilliard started back. Holgast stopped him.

"He's got his boots on. Was it him pacing the floor you heard, Shade?"

"No. More like crawling. Or scraping."

Hilliard frowned. "What the hell were you doing, Madigan?"

"You think he'd tell you?" Holgast asked. "I can hear him saying, 'Mr. Hilliard, sir, I was scraping a 'scape-hole with a knife I got hid in my boot!' "

Shade smiled faintly, but Hilliard raised the lamp again, his eyes searching the cross-hatched shadows that it cast into the cell. Twice he had Madigan move from one spot to another, and he kept shifting the lamp for a better view, but still he wasn't quite satisfied.

He asked Shade seriously, "D'you know if he packs a knife in his boot? I didn't think to search 'em."

Shade shrugged. "For all I know he could

pack a machete in his pants. I do know Holgast's put a bee in your bonnet. You won't rest easy till you find out. Got the key on you?"

"Yeah. Hold the lamp for me." Hilliard fished out his keys and inserted one in the lock. Before turning it, he said to Holgast, "Maybe you better hold your gun on him. He's a big feller, and if he's got a knife on him somewhere —"

"I was going to do that," Holgast said, and his drawling tone made Madigan give him first attention. Holgast, then, was the appointed executioner, giving him leave to pay off the score. He no longer carried his right arm in a sling, and had the use of it, but after drawing his gun he transferred it to his left hand.

The heavy door creaked open and Hilliard came into the cell, leaving it open. Madigan moved aside, watching Holgast; he caught a flicker of the eyes and a tightening of the mouth, and knew definitely that Holgast meant to kill him. Shade, holding up the lamp in his left hand, right hand resting on his hip, would come in on the play if needed.

From habit, Hilliard stepped first to the window and banged his hand testingly on the bars. Holgast's eyes followed him, then

162

slid to Madigan. For an instant both men stared at each other, the knowledge of coming murder flashing between them.

Shade lowered the lamp and raised it high again, making Madigan's shadow shift on the wall, and Holgast uttered his false yell of warning: "Look out, Hilliard!"

Madigan dived low at Hilliard's legs. Holgast's shot roared into the cell. He ripped the Dragoon .44 out from under his shirt as the marshal toppled on top of him with a startled howl, and fired from the floor a split-second after Holgast got off a second shot.

He heard Holgast's harsh intake of breath. Hilliard muttered something and rolled limply off him. Shade rapped at Holgast, "Dammit, you hit the marshal!" Shadows rushed back and forth, the lamp swaying, Shade making his draw and stepping in for a fast shot.

"The marshal hit *me!*" Holgast groaned, confused.

The lamp, meeting the top of the doorway, tilted in Shade's hand. In his haste Shade hadn't reckoned on the obstruction and he instinctively flung an upward look at it as he was on the point of firing. Madigan, too, raised a swift glance, cleared his gun above the moaning marshal, and pitched a shot at

163

the lamp. It had a brass base, unbreakable, but the glass chimney dissolved and the lighted wick dimmed smokily.

Shade dropped it, either fearing that it might explode over him or else promptly realizing that it was worse than useless to him as a light — the smoky flame marked him, but didn't reach to Madigan in the cell. It guttered and failed to go out. He jumped back, firing a blind shot and kicking the abused lamp into the cell.

"Come out o' there, Madigan!"

"Be right out!"

Madigan kicked it back into the passage. He tagged a bullet after it, scored a direct hit on the wick container, and a streak of burning oil spurted from its brass tank as it rolled wobbling over the floor. Holgast lurched off, sliding along the wall for support and begging Shade for help. Shade, retreating from the erratic spurts of burning oil, cursed him.

People could be heard already running in the street and shouting the alarm of a jail break. At the front door Mr. Focht bawled, "Jail's on fire! Form a bucket line!" It was like him to think first of saving the expense of building a new jail. "Shade! Where's Hilliard?"

"Madigan shot him!"

"Where'd he get the gun?"

Shade made an exasperated sound, grabbing Holgast and hauling him along. "He got a-hold o' one somehow! Shot Holgast, too!"

The passage filled with smoke. Madigan quit the cell crouched low and treading fast over burning patches. Snatching Hilliard's ring of keys from the lock, he took them to the rear end of the passage. The back door, never used by Hilliard, proved obstinate.

After he located the right key by trial and feel, the rusty lock jammed until he forced it to yield. The door refused to budge. He wrenched the handle off before discovering that it opened outward, and ramming his shoulder at it he burst it open and tumbled down two wooden steps into a dark and noisy night. Men were hurrying from all over town, and Mr. Focht kept on bawling for a bucket line.

Madigan pushed the door shut and broke into a sprint. His head was clear now. No trial for him. Shoot him down on sight. He heard the impatient stamp of a hoof, and angled toward the sound, slowing to a walk so as not to scare the horse. He figured it was in the livery yard, but a voice hailed him before he got there.

"Hey!" The man, mounted, sat holding his restive horse at halt alongside the livery stable. A white Stetson cut a pale silhouette in the darkness. "What's going on at the jail?"

"A fire," Madigan replied, muffling his voice. "Feller tried to break out." He covered his bandaged head with his hands as if stretching, and yawned, walking forward.

"Is he dead?"

He yawned again, and veered to come up behind the horse. It would be a good horse. Severne aimed to ride home as soon as Shade and Holgast did their task; he was only waiting until he knew for sure. It was important to him.

Severne asked again, "Is he dead?" — snapping the question and twisting around to look at Madigan, now close behind him. His shocked eyes rounded. He made a strange sound deep in his throat.

"Not yet," Madigan said, and leaped. The barrel of his gun crushed the white Stetson. He calculated it as a sense-shattering blow, but the big hat cushioned it. The horse shied.

Severne's thick body swayed, without losing rigidness, and his hands didn't drop the reins. He was staving off senselessness by the sheer power of his will, automatically retaining control of his horse. A groaning cry burst from him.

"Here he is! Here's Madigan!"

Madigan grasped at his coat and dragged him out of the saddle, tearing the reins from his hands. The horse, a tall dun, plunged, jerking to break away from him. He fought its head down, chased it in a tight circle, and on his second try he landed in the saddle.

Severne, both hands spread on the ground and his bowed head sinking, again uttered his furious cry. "Here's Madigan!"

The dun took off before Madigan found the stirrups or got the reins straightened out. It clattered into the main street with him and bolted up it, weaving to shake him off, a thoroughly upset horse.

Shots cracked from the front of the jail, where men were running in with buckets of water. Shade yelled, "Stop him! It's Madigan! He's — *Ho*-lee Jupe, he's took Severne's horse!"

A long-legged cowhand ran out at the dun. He missed his jump at its head, and clawed at the saddle. Madigan booted him in the chest. The dun went to pitching as it ran. Other men swarmed out into the street ahead. Blind with rage and terror, the dun humped its back and charged through them.

They scattered aside, whirling to blaze shots after it.

The hard jolting drove nails of agony into Madigan's injured head. He untangled the reins and leaned to swing off the street out of the gunfire, but the dun was too frenzied to obey neck-reining, so he reached forward and shortened rein, hauling its head over. That only caused it to stumble badly and break stride, recovering itself when almost to its knees.

A smashing blow in his right side shook a gasp from him. The reins slipped in his hands. He clutched the saddle horn and hung on, shuddering, straining to overcome the onslaught of sick blackness, to last through the first shock of a bad wound.

A man bellowed, "I hit him!"

The dun horse ran on, back in full stride, no longer pitching and weaving, its self-chosen course purposeful. The main street fell behind, and the houses on the fringe of town. The road stretched easterly, slanting toward north.

Madigan pushed at the saddle horn, forcing himself to sit upright. His body felt broken in the middle. Pain began, steadily increasing, defeating the numbness and prodding alive his reeling senses. He realized dimly that the dun was heading for home, running to its own familiar range; its *querencia.*

That would do. He didn't aim to pay a call on H 7, but the direction was right. Beyond H 7 range was the Pecos and the Romedy camp. Maybe the Romedy rawhiders would help him. Nobody else he could turn to. After all, he had gone out on a limb for Dare Romedy. Got her out of a scrape. Her folks might do as much for him. He needed help the worst way.

He couldn't twist his body, but he managed to look back over his shoulder. Riders were streaming out from the receding lights of Sanburn, coming hard after him. The dun wasn't the only good horse in the country. They knew he was hit, too damaged to attempt any longrider tricks of back-tracking and dodging them in the dark.

"I'm in a bad fix!" he muttered, and concentrated on reaching the Romedy camp, telling himself, yes, they'd help him.

If, came the thought, *I can find their trail down those high bluffs. If I can stay on this horse. If I don't bleed to death.*

The dun wanted to turn off to H 7. Its vitality spent, it lumbered at a heavy lope, but still uncorked a show of sullen temper. Madigan, his head splitting and his ribs on fire, mumbled curses, forcing the horse on toward the Pecos.

His pursuers hadn't got within shooting distance of him the whole way out, but at H 7 they could pick up fresh mounts. It meant a delay. On the other hand, they knew by now that he was making for the Romedy camp, so they'd race straight to the bluffs, no dallying to cut his sign.

He passed by the ghost village of Arruga, ruins of a few adobe-and-wattle *jacales* slowly disintegrating in a fold of hills. There the road bent southward. He left it and angled farther toward the north, relying on memory to give him his direction. The rising ground roughened to brushy hills slashed by arroyos that were too narrow to ride in and too wide for the dun to jump.

He was weak and, like the horse, spent. Worse, his eyes were failing him, making everything jiggle. It seemed an hour of zigzag climbing before he topped out on a plateau, the flat head of the bluffs overlooking the Pecos. He swore at the moon for rising at a time that was all wrong for him; it skylined him.

On the edge of the bluffs he reined the dun to a walk, searching for the trail down to the river. It had to be somewhere along here at the river's bend. He heard riders plunging up the hills, brisk sounds removing all doubt that they rode fresh horses. He kicked the dun to a trot, desperate to find the trail.

There was no sign of one. The bluffs were slanted walls, great rocky barriers sheering down to the Pecos, no bank visible below. His failing eyes had let him miss the trail. Or he had struck the bluffs too far upriver. Or Severne had lied and there wasn't any trail.

A voice called, "There he goes!"

The riders rose onto the plateau, immediately fanning out to trap him. He heeled the dun and along the edge of the bluffs, clinging to a dwindling hope of finding a trail down. The foremost riders opened fire. The range was somewhat long for six-guns, but the betraying moon made him a tempting target.

A bullet punched his shoulder. He yawed half out of the saddle, made a grab at the horn, and felt the dun jerk away under him. He saw, dead ahead, an inward cut of the bluff. The dun slid on braced forelegs, then floundered in its frantic effort to avoid skidding over the edge. Madigan missed his grab for the horn. He swung outward, unable to help himself or the horse.

He was falling through the air, the scream

of the horse in his ears. The face of the bluff slammed him off, and he lit again, rolling, rocks battering him.

Another fall, a bone-crackling impact, and his body stopped. It seemed as if the whole world had come to a standstill. The splash of the horse striking the river raised a whisper of echoes.

A distant voice said, "That's the last of *him!*"

Fragments of hazy consciousness came and went. Daylight pried at his closed eyelids, and passed on. He couldn't move, nor utter a sound. A slow, soft flutter came and went. Deep below the blankness of his mind he knew it to be a buzzard, and knew he was dying.

XIV

"We'd have to use ropes, with a couple of us carrying him. Then rig a stretcher. I don't know as it's worthwhile."

"It's worthwhile to me."

"How about him? In his shape, I don't believe I'd want to be —"

"He can't speak for himself. I'm speaking for him."

"Then we'll do what we can."

Hands touched him. He snarled silently. The meddling fools! Couldn't they see he was dead? The living core of him floated off yonder, nodding farewell, bearing away all the wracking pain. Damn them they'd try to drag him back and imprison him in this smashed body.

"He moved his lips."

"I think he's cussing us for bothering him. Wants to die in peace."

"He mustn't die."

"He's nearly gone. Nearly fooled the buzzards. Doubt if he can stand being moved."

"He mustn't die. . . ."

In the eternity that followed, Madigan's ears became familiar with that insistent voice: *"He mustn't die!"* And other voices at long intervals.

"That fall, after what he'd already taken — no wonder."

"Damaged his mind."

His mind was not damaged. It hovered somewhere outside of himself, like an escaped bird that was shy of the cage and yet reluctant to fly too far from it. He doggedly sought to recapture it, but it flitted off and eluded him.

He talked, shouted, cursed. He glared at vague figures about him. He tried to attack them.

"Getting his strength back."

"Have to strap him down."

They made him prisoner, regarded him with calm eyes, and went away shaking their heads. One remained, always, feeding him, caring for him, soothing his violent outbursts.

His mind at last gave up its truant freedom. Its return swept dark curtains from his eyes, restoring untricked vision and clarity. The senseless fury drained from him. He took stock of himself, struggling to establish the time and place, and to recall what had passed.

Leather straps, rawhide, held his arms and legs. They were fashioned to allow him limited movement, and were not uncomfortable. Much thought and care had gone into their making. He lay on a cot in a canvas-topped wagon that was fitted out for living in: a washbasin on a stand and a mirror over it; trunks; rawhide chairs; a bearskin rug.

A hand was in his own, held tightly. He stared up into the face of Dare Romedy. "You're real," he said slowly.

Glad triumph shone in her emerald eyes. "As real as you."

He loosened the tightness of his grip on her hand, afraid that he was hurting her. "You had to strap me down."

"To keep you from injuring yourself."

"I'm in your camp."

"Yes. In my wagon." She drew her hand from his, to work on the straps, freeing him, and moved back for him to rise from the cot.

He tested his arms and legs, stretched his back, discovering that he was not crippled. The scars interested him, there were so many. He wore only a clean shirt and flannel pants, not his own, and his feet were bare.

"I searched for your trail down the bluffs," he said, feeling as if it had happened only a few days ago.

She nodded, watching him understandingly. "You missed it by half a mile. We heard the shooting."

"I went over the edge. And my horse. Severne's horse. But you know that."

"Yes. We heard the men riding off afterwards. They thought you'd gone into the river with the horse. They thought they'd killed you."

"So did I!"

"So did we," she said. "The buzzards led us to you two days later. They were soaring low over you."

"I thank the buzzards." He padded to the mirror above the washbasin. The face in it

startled him. He had a thick beard. White
sears changed the shape of his eyebrows.
He turned and stared blankly at Dare Romedy.

"It's been a long summer," she told him
in answer to his unspoken question. "Hard
months for you."

"And for you."

"No. I knew some day you'd — find
yourself." Her eyes suddenly brimmed tears.
"I meant to keep you in my wagon until
you did — until you got well."

He stepped close to her. "You'd have gone
on taking care of me, no matter how long?"

"Of course I would."

"Feeding me, washing me, all the jobs a
nurse has to do for a man who can't do for
himself?"

She smiled, wiping her tears. "You don't
know women."

He took her in his arms, and she pressed
to him readily, tilting her face to his, her
hands sliding strongly about him. He heard
her heart pounding like his own. His demanding hands plucked at her dress. She
gasped, kissed him fiercely, and pulled away
from him.

Breathless, not hiding her regret, she
whispered, "The folks are outside. Let's go
tell them you're a whole man again."

"That I am!" he said with straight force.

Her husky little laugh bubbled shakily. "I'm glad!"

"And you're a whole woman."

"That I am!"

The Romedys had dark hair, with the exception of two or three of the women who had married into the clan. In most other ways, too, they differed from the Trubbidges.

The men shaved, or kept their beards trimmed, and they weren't forever spitting tobacco juice. Rich of mood and fluent of speech when occasion called, reticent betweentimes, they wore the restraint of men who could be coolly dangerous. They owned good big wagons, nothing ramshackle, and a herd of fine horses. The women dressed decently, did up their hair, and knew how to cook a meal and set a table. The children didn't run around half naked and in need of soap.

Madigan shook hands, beginning with old Jaffah Romedy, head of the clan, a white-bearded patriarch whose austere manner didn't quite go with his humorous eyes. And Shep Romedy, son of Jaffah, a fifty-year-old edition of his father. And Blair, Jared, Duncan — sons of Shep and his wife Katherine.

More than a dozen others, including one they called Silent Lionel, whose exact relationship Madigan couldn't place, but who obviously was a Romedy, gravely welcomed him back to life and sanity. He had an odd feeling of making fresh acquaintance with people whom he had known for a long time.

He laid his sense of familiarity to the fact that he had been living among them for months, although without having had much consciousness of them. Shallow impressions, perhaps, had been imprinted on his memory. But it went deeper than that. It was more like a sense of kinship, of understanding that needed no words.

He moved among them, was one of them, accepted and unquestioned. His own clothes had been washed and mended, his boots repaired, gun cleaned and oiled. Someone had provided him with a hat. As a single man he ate with whichever family group invited him; an invitation was never lacking.

At night he slept beneath Dare's wagon, not knowing who provided the blankets — they were simply there for him to use. By day he helped work with the herd of horses, whose training went on constantly. He thought he knew how to handle horses, but the Romedy men quietly taught him a few things. The blacks were not cow ponies. They were blooded animals, high-spirited. They called for gentle handling. Not one of them bore a scar.

He got around finally to asking questions that bothered him. In the evening, while the women washed supper dishes and put the younger children to bed, the custom of the men was to gather at old Jaffah's fire, light up smokes, and discuss the progress of various horses.

During a lull, Madigan said, "This is about as safe a camp as I've seen. Just one trail up the bluffs, easily guarded. The river's risky to cross here."

"Except on the raft," Shep's son Duncan said. "We built it to ferry the wagons across."

"I've looked at it. It's a brute. Doesn't appear to've been used lately." Madigan paused to choose his words. "The only cattle I've seen here is that little bunch you raise for your own beef. And yet —" He spread his hands.

"And yet what?" Duncan asked companionably. "Spill it out, Jim."

"It doesn't tie in with that they say about you."

Shep took it up. "What they say about us is what Henry Severne wants 'em to say,

179

and what they want to believe. We'd be strangers here if we stayed forty years. Outsiders. None of us men could go into Sanburn and not have to fight to get out. So Dare goes in when we need supplies. And they even gave her some trouble once, as you well know."

"Why d'you let it go on?"

"Their lies?" Shep shrugged. "Not worth trying to stop. We'll be moving on before long."

"Where to?" Madigan asked, and Shep glanced queryingly at his father, mutely asking if Madigan had the right to know.

Old Jaffah tamped his pipe, gazing at Madigan's face. "A far piece," he said. "Along our way there'll be people who'll drop everything when they see us coming — people who know what a Romedy horse is, and willing to pay our price for any we care to sell. It's our living. The Romedys have been raising these blacks since before I was born."

Pride lent him a strong touch of austerity. He kept his eyes on Madigan.

"We maintain our standards. We live the way we like to live, free to roam, free of the nuisances of land ownership, petty laws and officials, and the prying of inquisitive neighbors," he said, once more displaying the

Romedy flair for fluent speech. "In some parts of the country, such as here, the people regard us as disreputable and worse."

Madigan nodded. "Rawhiders."

"Yes. We use rawhide a good deal. We live pretty much like rawhiders, and we get along with those we meet. People think they've got to pin a label on us." Old Jaffah smiled. "You don't find that hard to understand. From what I hear, they pinned a label on the Madigans."

"I'd trade it for your kind of rawhider," Madigan said. "But I think you should put a stop to letting them label you as thieves."

"Why should we try? It would draw us into their petty affairs, the last thing we want."

"The calf rustling isn't petty," Madigan argued. "Henry Severne's doing it to break the small ranchers and take over their holdings. He wants those springs for insurance against drought."

Jaffah shrugged. "It's not our concern, as long as they leave us alone. Let them fight it out among themselves. Let them call us anything. We're free of all that. And they do leave us alone, never fear. Some of Severne's riders once prowled down the bluffs at night, trying a raid on our horses."

He smiled. The deceptively mild faces of

the men around the fire reflected his smile.

"Silent Lionel met them with his rifle. He was guarding the trail that night, and didn't trouble to send down an alarm to the rest of us. He shot three of them. We've had no unwelcome visitors since then."

Silent Lionel went on smoking, his gaze faraway as if he had not heard. His manner was habitually that of a man in deep meditation, undisturbed by passing events. Yet in him, too, as in the others, could be sensed a quietly fierce presence. They were self-sufficient.

Madigan said, "But you carried me here to your camp and took care of me. You took me in, a stranger."

Jaffah knocked out his pipe, while the other men stayed silent to let him speak for them. "You were not unwelcome, man. We would have welcomed you any time since the day you took up for Dare in Sanburn. Dare was orphaned when she was a little girl. She belongs to all of us. If you hadn't shot Holgast — if he had laid the quirt on her — we would've had to go in and attend to it. No knowing what that could've led to. You put us all in your debt."

Hearing her name spoken, Dare came over to the fire. Madigan said, "The debt was paid. Somebody pushed a gun through my cell window. I broke jail with it. This gun." He tapped the butt of the Dragoon .44 in his holster.

The men's eyes went to Dare. "So?" Shep murmured. "We know that gun. Don't we, Dare?"

She nodded, smiling. "Mine. I did it. I'd do more than that for him, gladly — much more," she told them, and walked off to her wagon.

Shep broke the group's silence, murmuring again, "So?" He looked at Madigan. "There's nothing much for us in these parts. We stayed here mostly because she seemed set on it and hated to leave. Made me wonder if she'd finally met a man who suited her. She's never had a man. I hoped he'd be our kind."

"We met one night in the Trubbidge camp," Madigan said. "She was out hunting a stray horse."

"Must've been before we found this spot. That was quite awhile back."

"Yes. The Trubbidges are long gone."

"It was about that time she began taking a fancy to these parts." Shep's tone was dry. "If we'd known why —"

"I never forgot her, but things happened. I wasn't free to search for her. Didn't even know she was still in the country, till I was

183

told some rawhiders named Romedy were camped on the Pecos."

"You're free now."

"I'm wanted on a list of charges," Madigan said slowly. "Shooting Holgast. Rustling. Jail-break. Maybe murder. Do I have any right to —"

"Nobody's looking for you," Shep interrupted him. "Jim Madigan's been officially dead for months."

Madigan gazed around at the faces of the group. "Does that mean I'm still welcome among you?"

For answer, Jaffah said, "We ferry the wagons over, and cross the river again any place it's shallow. Down through the Big Bend, into Mexico at about Castolon — the *dons* pay anything for a fine horse — through Chihuahua and Sonora to Arizona, where we've got customers. Then on to California. The Californios pay well, too. Might push on up to Canada this time, but anyhow we'll swing over to Montana and Wyoming." He stopped, and asked abruptly, "Is Madigan an Irish name?"

"I guess it is." Madigan's mind reached into early memory. "I can remember my great-grandfather. He called himself Black Irish. I think he had some Spanish blood in him from way back. God knows how old he was, but he had an itching foot and was forever going off somewhere. Come to think of it, we were all restless, the lot of us."

"We're Irish and Welsh. Never settled long anywhere and most likely never will. What d'you think on that route? It'll be years before we strike Texas again."

"When do we start?" Madigan asked, and all the faces smiled. For a moment the brooding meditation lifted from the eyes of Silent Lionel, the nerveless slayer.

"The sooner the better," Shep murmured, and heads nodded.

They were nomads, like the far-wandering horse breeders and herdsmen of ancient days, despising roofs and the tame comforts of home life, refusing to settle down any-where for long. Madigan again felt that sense of kinship with them, along with a feeling of having lived among aliens before finally finding his own people.

XV

"We'll soon be leaving this place," he told Dare.

"I know," she said, shining-eyed. "I have to ride to Sanburn tomorrow for supplies — coffee especially. We drink a lot of coffee when we're on the road, you'll find. My last trip to Sanburn! The last time I'll ever have to go anywhere alone."

They stood in darkness by her wagon. At some time they had started to bid each other goodnight. In the meantime the campfires had burned out. The camp was hushed, sleeping, all but the night guard somewhere on the trail up the bluffs.

"Do you know what *querencia* means?" he asked her. She shook her head, knowing little Spanish. "To a Mexican it means his favorite place, the place where his heart is. Sometimes it means the place he hopes some day to find."

" 'The place where his heart is,' " she echoed. "Meaning happiness."

"Happiness and contentment, yes. I searched years for mine. I never found it."

"Of course you didn't."

"Why do you say that?"

"Because happiness isn't a place," she said simply.

The calm statement was a revelation to him. He pondered on it. She was right, dead right. How blind could a man be? He laughed. "*Mi querencia está aquí!* Do you know what *vida mia* means?"

"Yes. It means 'my life'."

"When a man whispers it to a woman, or

186

she to him, it means something else. Like *mi corazon* — 'my heart'."

"*Vida mia,*" she whispered. "*Mi corazon. . . .*"

She came into his arms, pressing to him, holding him strongly, her face to his. Unrestrained, his hands caressed her, growing quickly bold. She shivered, her warm breath fast. "Our wagon," she whispered, yielding unashamed, and he lifted her up and bore her into the wagon.

Dare returned from her trip to Sanburn next day at dusk. She was very quiet, her manner toward Madigan almost shy during supper. The men appeared not to notice. The women, wisely gentle, were aware that she had realized her rich capacity for passion; she was shaken by vivid memories.

"You're not eating your fill, Dare."

"I'm not hungry."

A woman passed her the coffee. "After that tiring ride?"

"It wasn't too bad. Seemed longer, though."

It would seem longer, said the eyes of the women. A whole day away from your man. Tremulous at the overwhelming passion that he could arouse in you, half aghast at its utter abandon, but hurrying eagerly back to him. They knew the Romedy temperament and nature. She had it in full measure, a strong and healthy girl full of newly kindled fire.

"I think I'll go to bed early," she said, not meeting Madigan's eyes. "Goodnight, all."

She waited for him that night at the wagon, bride-like and glowing.

From her manner during supper he thought something might have happened on her trip to Sanburn, and later he asked her, "What goes on around town? Anything changed?"

She shook her head, cradled on his shoulder. "Nothing much that you wouldn't expect. Henry Severne is the big man, and everybody kowtows to him. Hilliard quit — yes, he recovered — and Severne put in Redlinger as town marshal. Shade will run for county sheriff, against Calhoun, with Severne's backing. He already acts as if he's won the election, as no doubt he will."

"And the calf rustling, does it still go on?"

"There aren't many calves left to rustle! The small ranchers are desperate. It's high time we moved on. Let's talk about us." She chuckled in his ear. "When are you going to ask me to marry you?"

"Now. Will you marry me?"

"Yes!"

"That's settled," he said. "Has Severne

taken over any of the small ranchers' holdings yet?"

"No. Dr. Osborne has been buying their notes and mortgages as they fell due, and extending them more time. How many children shall we have?"

"I don't know, but I bet we make an early start." He began suspecting that she wanted to sidetrack him off the subject of Sanburn and its doings. "Severne must be mad at the doctor for doing that. It crosses him up. They were getting to be sort of friendly together. But of course the doctor doesn't know the game Severne's playing. Are they still on good terms?"

"Apparently. What shall we name our first? It will be a boy. We Romedy women bear mostly boys. Have you noticed how they outnumber the girls?"

He knew then that she was being evasive. "Severne was actually trying to court Arabella," he said, and instantly felt her stiffen. "He wanted to marry her. Can you believe it?"

He heard her swallow before saying, "Yes, I can believe it, Jim."

"How is she?"

She sighed, giving up any further attempt to dissemble. "Miss Arabella Truebridge," she pronounced distinctly, "is doing very well for herself, with the blessing of Dr. Osborne who believes Henry Severne will give her solid security."

"What?" Madigan sat bolt upright. "Dare, is that true?"

"I wish it wasn't. I wish I hadn't gone to Sanburn today. It's all over town. People are there from all over the county. I didn't want to tell you. I was afraid. They're getting married tonight — a big wedding at the doctor's house."

Her words stunned him into a long silence. She touched his arm. "Does it mean so much to you, Jim?"

"I've got to stop it," he said heavily. "Got to warn her."

"Oh, why did you make me tell you?" she cried. "Why didn't I lie? Jim, you can't go!"

"I have to. He's a thief, a crook, a killer! He'd make her life a living hell!"

"You're not responsible!"

"I am! I took her away from him once. I as good as killed my best friend because of her. She was his girl, and when he died I took on the responsibility to take care of her. She's where she is because I put her there!"

"You've paid your obligation," Dare insisted.

"Not if I let her marry Severne," he said.

"I know him too well! She'd be far better off back in the Trubbidge camp — better off if I'd let Jay shoot her! How could I live with myself? Jay would haunt me all my life. Don't you see I've got to go?"

Her frantic opposition crumbled. "Yes, but — Oh, I'm so afraid of losing you! Let some of the men go with you."

He shook his head. "It's purely my concern. I can't dodge it, and I can't drag them into it. I won't try."

"But they'll kill you in Sanburn!"

"I've been killed. They won't know me behind this beard. I'll shave it off when I get back."

"If" — her voice broke — "if you get back!"

He couldn't make light of the risk. It was there and they both knew it. To pretend otherwise would be foolish. "As long as I live," he told her, "I'll come back to you if I have to crawl clear across Texas."

"Your words are sweet, Jim, but what you're doing is bitter to me."

He held her to him, wordless, knowing her anguish, then asked, "Can I borrow a horse?"

"Take mine." She rose. "I'll help you saddle."

They went out and quietly saddled the

black, and walked with it to the trail that steeply ascended the bluffs. A dog ran out to them beneath one of the silent wagons, but didn't bark. The Romedys allowed few dogs in camp. Those they had were trained to behave themselves around horses. Dare patted the dog and it amiably followed behind her.

Torrents of words struggled for expression in Madigan. There were so many things he had left unsaid to her, letting his actions speak for him. He hadn't even told her that he loved her, in words, leaving it to be taken for granted. He opened his mouth to speak.

She said to him, "I feel like I'm helping you on your way to another woman, damn her!"

It diverted what he had about to say. "Don't be bitter at Arabella," he begged her. "To me she's like a child that I picked up — a lost and homeless child."

"She's not a child now!"

"Not in some ways," he admitted, "but in other ways — well, I don't think of her as a grownup."

"Are you sure?" she asked, low-voiced, her eyes on the path. "You must know how hard it is for a woman to trust her man's protective instinct when it's aimed at another woman. You and she were together a lot.

She was possessive toward you. I saw it in her face. She tied you down, wouldn't let you go."

"I've told you why I still can't let her get hurt," he said a bit sharply.

They were edging toward a quarrel, and hating it, dismayed that it should happen at this time, at any time. She turned swiftly to him, her face wet with tears.

"Make me believe it! Oh, Jim, please — make me believe it! Tonight I'm a jealous woman, God help me!"

A figure stepped out onto the dark path ahead of them. "What goes on?" It was Duncan Romedy, Shep's youngest son, on night guard. "That you, Dare?"

Madigan heard Dare draw a long breath to steady herself. "Yes. It's all right. Jim Madigan's with me. I'm seeing him up the trail. He has to go off for — for something."

Young Duncan moved down closer to them. " 'Lo, Jim; where you going? Funny time o' night to start out. What's the rush?"

"We'll be moving on soon," Madigan said. "It's something that won't wait. Something I've got to do first."

"Oh. Personal business."

"Yeah."

" 'Scuse me." Duncan stepped aside, his rifle dangling in one hand. He wasn't stupid.

None of the Romedys were stupid. He was young, though, given to virile night-dreamings that disregarded the dreams and desires of others. "I'll see Jim the rest of the way up, Dare," he said obligingly. "You can go on back."

"Thank you, Duncan." She could have killed him.

"You're welcome. Come on, Jim."

Leading the dainty-stepping black and walking on up the trail with Duncan, Madigan looked back. All he got was a blurred outline of Dare in the dark, and the dog, standing there, watching him go. The presence of Duncan had prohibited the clinging farewell and the warm assurance. *God,* he prayed, *let me come back to her. Let me prove to her that she's all that matters in my life. I never lived till now.*

"Here we are!" Duncan proclaimed cheerfully. "Top o' the trail, Jim. Hurry back!"

"I'll do that. Thanks, Duncan."

"Tonight I'm a jealous woman." I'm a jealous man, Dare. I'll kill any man who tried to take you from me. Any time. You are mine. As long as I live you are mine.

He had no time to spare if Arabella's marriage was to take place at midnight, maybe earlier. Sanburn wasn't an all-night cow-town since Hilliard's rule. But Hilliard was

194

gone. Redlinger, the new town marshal, Severne's man, would certainly change the rules to suit Severne. Throw the town side-open this night. Big wedding. Whole county invited. Henry Severne was taking a wife. Old bull had got himself a fresh young heifer. No hurry, he'd breed her on H 7 where ears ignored screams.

An hour's ride west of the ghost village of Arruga, Madigan heard a sustained grumble of sound, so familiar to cattle country that in his urgent preoccupation he hardly noticed it. In a minute the thought intruded that a dark night was no time to be driving a herd of cattle. A stampede, more likely. No cowman in his right senses would start a drive this late in the year, anyway, unless it was a short drive; in which case he wouldn't be in such a rush. Those cattle were running. A mountain lion or prowling coyotes must have spooked them.

He heard the sound again miles farther on, and, paying it closer attention, he pulled the racing black up for a breather and listened. Another running herd, far off and seemingly headed northward. This time, at halt with nothing to interrupt his hearing, he distinguished occasional thin cries of hazing riders. If it was a stampede, it was man-made. He touched the black horse on-ward.

The rumble of a third herd reached him before he struck the stretch of level road running through the flat range that sur-rounded Sanburn. Here and there at widely separated points the sky reflected faint red-dish glows, like the sullen warning of Sioux fires he had seen up on the North Platte when he had once ridden scout for a wagon train.

Things were happening tonight — burn-ings, and a hasty exodus of cattle. He shrugged, telling himself impatiently that it wasn't his concern what ruination blighted this country. Its people had outlawed him unjustly. What was happening in Sanburn, at Dr. Osborne's house, and what would happen when he got there, made their troubles unimportant.

Arabella. He thought of her as she had stood on the portico of Severne's big ranch house, in that rose-colored dress, blocking Severne's shotgun and then stepping clear for Severne to take a bullet through his arm. A rawhider girl.

And now she would marry the man. Poor Jay would turn in his grave there under the pecans within sight and sound of the big house. A hideous evil. Dr. Osborne must have exerted strong influence over her, helped mightily by Severne's overpowering will. Surely she couldn't have changed that much, inside.

XVI

Noise issued from the lighted barroom and lobby of the Sanburn Hotel & Bar, an overflowing crowd jostling in front. Every hitchrack space on the street was occupied, late-arriving horses and rigs tied up to anything handy.

The end of the summer work, and continued fine weather, had brought everybody into town from miles around to attend the wedding. Ranchers and their womenfolk, dressed in Sunday best, mingled with people of the town, groups bursting into the easy laughter of a holiday mood. Price's Emporium and Focht's General Merchandise had lighted lamps placed in their windows as a courtesy to the crowd, but they couldn't compete with the Osborne house, where every window blazed and colored lanterns hung on posts in front.

The livery was still open. Madigan checked in the lathered black for a rubdown. A busy liveryman said, "I'll try to get somebody on it. Needs it. You musta come in a hurry, stranger."

"I did."

"You hit our town at a mighty big time. Big weddin'. Biggest man in the county gettin' married."

"Sounds big."

He left the livery and threaded his way past shifting groups along the street to the Osborne house. In the pack of humanity at the open front door he saw a few faces of men he remembered, ranchers and townsmen in white shirts dampened by perspiration under heavy broadcloth. No man ever knew why women didn't suffocate in the voluminous dresses and petticoats. It wasn't stylish to show discomfort. They smiled bright smiles and trilled endless chatter, sipping from glass goblets, little fingers elegantly extended.

He pushed through to the door and edged into the front hall. Here the pack was a little looser, but not much, the close air warmed by body heat and odorous with the scent of wine, tobacco, flowers, and whatever it was that women put on themselves which men did not.

People he brushed by ran disapproving looks over his range garb, hat, and bearded face. None of the eyes showed recognition, but men took frowning note that he was wearing a gun — a serious breach of etiquette in any Sanburn social gathering, especially a wedding. A man might carry a small arsenal on his person, ranging from an armpit gun to a two-shot derringer carried in his pants pocket along with his loose change, but to bring a gun nakedly into a mixed gathering was bad social form. He saw Shade's hawk-nosed face, the eyes narrowed at him.

Shade wore his gun, but he had the right as a deputy sheriff on duty. And Redlinger, town marshal since Hilliard had quit. They flanked the door to the parlor where, from the popping of champagne corks and babble of voices, the main festivities were taking place.

"Hold it, you!" Redlinger barred Madigan from pssing on through. "Who d'you think you are?"

Looking over him into the parlor, Madigan didn't reply. It required no extensive experience of formal weddings to realize the stage that this one had reached. Women, nibbling cake, flocked around a table piled with gifts, the gist of their chatter having it that this was the grandest wedding in Sanburn's history, this the finest wedding cake they had ever tasted. Men, jovial at the refreshments table, clinked glasses in unorganized toasts to the bride and groom.

The church minister fiddled with a glass of champagne, undecided about the propriety of his drinking it in public; he preached temperance as a virtue, confusing it with total abstinence. Dr. Osborne and Sheriff Calhoun wore swallow-tail coats, making clear their functions: the doctor had given the bride away, and the sheriff had stood as best man — an honor that must have surprised Calhoun.

Henry Severne stood smiling with Arabella at the head of the refreshments table, near the arched doorway that led to the rest of the house, shaking hands with those who still pressed around to congratulate him. He heartily urged them to make free with the bottles, laughed at men's jokes, and showed a willingness to make the wedding reception last all night.

In her white bridal gown Arabella looked the perfect bride, regal, serenely proud of herself. A bit pale, but if uneasy apprehensions pricked her they were salved by the knowledge of the high station she had achieved as wife of the big man of the county. On her left hand a diamond ring sparkled, next to a gold band.

They were married. It was done and over. Madigan searched Arabella's face for signs of regret. He saw only the pride. She *had* changed that much. It made her look older. He couldn't think of her as a child any longer — a rawhider waif who happened to have a gift for adapting herself to changed surroundings. She had learned fast, but thoroughly, and the lessons had remade her. She was a woman of ambition, satisfied to marry a rich man and attain a prominent position. Satisfied for now, at least. Later she would discover the emptiness of her bargain.

Drinks were going around. Henry Severne had proposed a toast. Everyone had to join in, no exceptions allowed. Somebody handed Madigan a filled glass. He looked at it, raised it, and his eyes went back to Arabella.

"To the bride," he said, "God help her!" He had not consciously intended to add that. It slipped out.

Henry Severne, about to give his toast, frowningly lowered his glass, demanding, "Who said that?"

Shade prodded a forefinger at Madigan's

chest. "You mean 'God bless her,' don't you?"

"Do I?"

The chattering and laughter stilled, an uncomfortable pall falling over the guests as if an embarrassing fact had been spoken that everyone wished to conceal. Arabella sent Madigan a haughtily offended stare. Henry Severne moved around the long table toward him.

"Do I know you? There's something about you that — Shade, who is he?"

"I don't call him to mind. Think I've seen him somewhere, though. Who invited you, feller?"

"Nobody."

"Where you from?"

"That doesn't matter," Madigan said. "I'm leaving."

"Good thing!"

"But first I want a word with the county sheriff."

"Oh?" Shade's eyelids flickered slightly. "What about?" He tapped the badge pinned to his shirt pocket. "I'm a deputy."

"I'll talk to the top man," Madigan said. "In private." Redlinger had moved around to stand behind him, and Shade's hand hung brushing his holster.

Hearing them, Sheriff Calhoun snapped,

"If you've got a complaint to make, tell it to Shade." His words betrayed the waning of his authority. Evidently realizing it, he thrust out his jaw, attempting a stern pose that failed to rise above irritable uncertainty.

Madigan checked him out of reckoning as a strong and dependable force. Calhoun no longer represented the spear-head in county law enforcement. He was an aging has-been, due to get voted out of office. The swallow-tail coat, a bad fit, lent him the forlorn aspect of a ruffled fowl. Shade was top man in all but title, and that he was sure to win. Maybe the county deserved him.

One recourse was left. A perilous one. "What I've got to say," Madigan began, "concerns —"

Severne didn't allow him to go further. "Friends, can a saddle-tramp stomp into my wedding party, here in Dr. Osborne's house, and shoot off his mouth? It's an insult to the doctor, to my bride, and to me! To all of us!"

"It concerns a lot of folks here." Madigan swept a look over those around him. They returned him looks of hostile scorn, resentment, anything but tolerance of an intruding stranger. He shrugged, knowing better than to spill what he had to say right here. *They* hadn't changed. "Anybody who's interested, follow me outside. It'd be to your advantage, not mine."

"What bill of goods d'you suppose he's trying to sell?" Severne loudly asked Dr. Osborne, and the doctor compressed his lips, annoyed by the unseemly incident.

"Let's go," Redlinger said at Madigan's back. "I'll follow you."

"What does that mean?" Madigan asked him over his shoulder.

"Means I'm town marshal and I'm runnin' you out o' town!"

"I'm getting out. Don't waste your time."

"I won't!"

Madigan helped the liveryman finish rubbing down the black, and saddled it. The ride back to the Romedy camp would have to be more leisurely than the ride in, in order not to overtax the horse. His trip had accomplished nothing, but he had tried; his conscience was clear. You couldn't very well save a woman who didn't want saving, nor warn men who wouldn't listen.

Redlinger, despising to walk any distance at all in tight boots, had borrowed a saddle horse. He eyed the black sharply, but said nothing about it, intent upon his purpose, which Madigan quickly learned was to put him squarely in front. Madigan set himself to thwart that design.

It became a contest of craft and guile, complicated by moving groups of men, rigs standing in the street, and a fist-fight. By the time they got to the edge of town Redlinger's horse was nervously unhappy, and the black, abreast, kept sidling to kick at it.

"Thanks for your company," Madigan murmured. He reined up.

Redlinger did the same. "I'll go a ways yet. Make sure you're gone."

"Appreciate it."

They walked their mounts slowly on, still keeping abreast, each taking care not to advance a pace ahead of the other. Redlinger sat his saddle a little stiffly, reins in his left hand, right hand on his thigh.

He's braced, Madigan mused. Out here in the dark is where he figured to do it, outside of town, only he thought he'd be behind me from the start. He knows I know it. I didn't get to say what I wanted to say back there, but I said too much. Severne or Shade gave him the sign. Well, then, he'll try a side-play, something to throw me off. . . .

Both horses shied, ears pricked at another horse standing patiently in the road before them. The horse nickered softly to them and they answered with snorts. It bore a saddle, no rider. For a second, waiting as he was for Redlinger to make a side-play of some kind, Madigan thought it a plant to distract him, and in that second he drew his gun.

Somebody groaned. A dark bundle lay under the riderless horse. Redlinger's right hand moved, and Madigan stabbed his gun at him, but Redlinger was taking aim at the dark bundle. Madigan hit him with a sweep of his arm.

"What the hell are you doing? The man's hurt! Put that gun away!"

Redlinger stared at him. He holstered his gun, dismounted, and hurried forward to the horse and its fallen rider. Madigan got to him as he was rolling the injured man roughly over onto his back, letting the head bump the hard ground. The man groaned again.

"You sonofabitch!" Madigan shouldered him away. "Give me a match!" Redlinger did nothing, said nothing, and Madigan tipped up his gun. "A match, damn you!" He felt for the match that Redlinger tossed to him, found it, and struck it alight.

The injured man was old, like his skinny nag, and shabby in broken boots and much-mended clothes. His unshaven face had the gray pallor of a corpse. "Who is he?" Madigan asked, and Redlinger still didn't speak.

"He's been shot a couple times. Who are you, old-timer?"

"Runnin' off all the cows." The old man's eyes stayed closed. "They're burnin' . . ." He sighed tiredly.

"He's off his head," Redlinger muttered.

"The hell he is! Give me a hand with him."

"What for? He's finished."

"We'll get him to the doctor. Give me a hand, or there'll be two of you!"

They lifted him onto his horse and, holding him on between them, packed him into town, Madigan keeping watch on Redlinger every step of the way. After a brief spell of brooding, Redlinger asked him a question.

"D'you believe what he said?"

"I know it for a fact."

"Hunh! Yeah, I guess you do."

They rode through the main street, rolling up a crowd behind them. At the Osborne house Madigan lifted the old man off his horse and carried him in, Redlinger stalking ahead to clear the way. The commotion brought the wedding party out of the parlor, causing a jam in the hall. Blocked, Madigan laid his burden on a hall sofa, ruining the plush with bloodstains.

Several people exclaimed that the old man was Sam Coble. Their tones implied that Sam Coble wasn't of much account, and

207

one woman went so far as to bewail the bloodstains. A cattleman then announced that as an act of charity he had hired old Sam to dig a spring tank and given him a place to sleep, provided he stayed reasonably sober.

"I was even going to pay him a little cash, 'sides his keep. That's me. I'll never get rich. How'd he get hurt?"

"Don't look like you get that spring tank dug, Prawn."

"I ain't about to pay for his doctorin', tell you that!"

No, they hadn't changed. They were part and parcel of a closed community, grown meanly intolerant in isolation, preserving cold standards of values drained dry of kindness and sympathy. Severne broke through the jam, Dr. Osborne in his wake, and confronted Madigan. "What's this you've done?" he demanded. He sent a hard look at Redlinger. "What happened?"

"Old Sam Coble's been shot. Tried to ride in, didn't make it." Redlinger shifted his eyes, guiding Severne's stare to Madigan. "We found him layin' out there on the road. Me an' him."

Madigan asked the doctor, "Want me to carry him to your office?"

Dr. Osborne, straightening up from a brief

examination, shook his head. "I'm afraid it's too late. This man is dead."

Sheriff Calhoun and Shade pushed through the tightly packed mob of guests. "Who shot old Sam?" Calhoun asked, and again there was that tinge of indifference carrying the implication that an old drunkard didn't rate as a citizen and a fellow human.

"Cow thieves," Redlinger answered him, but looked at Shade. "He told me the Romedy are out on the raid tonight — big raid — stealin' and burnin'."

"You're a liar!" Madigan snapped. "He said nothing about the Romedys! Not one of 'em has left their camp tonight."

Henry Severne swung to him. "How d'you know that? Eh? Who the devil are you?"

"Oh, he'd know," Redlinger said. "He knew the raid was on. Let it slip out to me when I asked him did he believe what old Sam had said. He wants to cover up for his friends."

"His friends? Who is he?"

"That I don't rightly know. Like Shade said too, I've got a hunch we've met before — the way he acts and talks, things like that. But there's one thing I do know about him. One thing that sets him spang in his place!" Redlinger paused to gain full attention.

XVII

The hushed crowd broke into a babble, those within hearing in the hall relaying garbled news of the raid, those outside pushing in to gather more information. Struck by the dismaying realization that their own livestock might be involved, ranchers cast away decorum in a rush to vacate the house and race home. They rammed into those who were trying to enter. Furniture crashed.

In his fullest voice Henry Severne bellowed, "Hold it, friends, hold it — don't waste your time scattering out all over the county! If the Romedys are running off cattle, we'll form a posse and hit their camp before they can cross the river. Shade, list all the men you can! Calhoun, arrest that feller!"

By the force of his personality he made them listen to him. He was taking charge, shaping order out of disorder, guiding their angry consternation into the channel of his choosing. A sharp-witted opportunist, he would not allow premature alarm of the raid to upset his overall purpose.

Through it all, Shade and Redlinger maneuvered together to close in on Madigan. In the swirling mob of men and woman, gunplay was out of the question. Calhoun joined them to make it a three-cornered team of stalkers, but at Severne's order to gather a posse Shade dropped out to obey. Having a low opinion of Calhoun as a rough-house wrestler, Redlinger then pulled his gun, disregardful of the risk of accidents.

Madigan dived into the crowd of guests who had swarmed out from the parlor. Bowling over several shouting men and screaming women, he plunged on through to the hall staircase and bobbed up on the third stair. A large bronze urn filled with a decorative display of tall peacock feathers graced the massive newel post of the oak bannisters. He used it as partial cover, in the absence of anything better.

He stroked out his gun and fired up at the ceiling.

His dive through the crowd had shaken the attention off Severne, and the shot transferred it definitely to him. He clinched it by saying, "I don't want to shoot where there are women, but if I have to — Redlinger, lower that gun!"

From the stairs he had full view of the

hall and its occupants. The men stilled, watching his gun. He banked on the presence of their womenfolk to restrain them from risking gunfire as long as they were not pushed too far. Their discretion afforded him that single margin of advantage. Playing it for all it was worth, he spoke to Calhoun, who stood close by Redlinger; an ill-matched pair. Calhoun had arrived there by making a vain grab at Madigan and blundering into Redlinger's line of fire.

"Stand away from him, Sheriff!"

Calhoun thrust down Redlinger's half-raised gun, and stamped to the foot of the staircase. "Don't tell me what to do! You're under arrest!"

Madigan dipped a glance at him and returned to his ranging survey of the hall, noting the effect of Sheriff Calhoun's unexpected resurgence of high-handed authority. Much of the wrathy frustration lifted from the faces of the men. They were long accustomed to Calhoun's effectively brow-beating manner of dealing with wrongdoers. Calhoun was seizing the opportunity to prove that he was as capable as ever, and from habit they were ready to lend him a hand if needed.

To halt the rapid shrinking of his slim and temporary advantage, Madigan rapped harshly, "Don't anybody try a crack at me! I'll nail him! Back off, Sheriff!"

It stopped Calhoun. He didn't back off, but neither did he advance any farther up the stairs. With one foot planted on the bottom tread, in a pose that gave him an incongruously casual air, he exchanged bullying for what he considered was reasonableness.

"Man, don't you see you can't get out of this house without I take you out under arrest? Now give me your gun and let's go, or you're in for bad trouble!"

Shade drawled aloud, "Listen to the ol' mossback playin' it safe!" His uplifted eyebrows asked Henry Severne for permission to do it his way.

Severne looked around at the crowded hall. He flattened his hand in a staying gesture to Shade, moving away from him, and said benevolently, "Ladies, I think you better leave till we get this ironed out. Doctor, would you kindly show the ladies to the other rooms?"

"I've got something to say," Madigan told Calhoun. "This time you'll listen. You'll all listen! Those cattle raiders —"

"Get on with it, Calhoun!" Severne called. "Take him if you're going to — we don't have all night to listen to you and him spout

213

off! You're showing your age!"

Calhoun flinched, sensitive to criticism, his age a particularly tender spot. He had heard Shade's sneering comment, as he was intended to, and Severne's gibe struck brutally at his freshly-found assurance. The garnering of votes to carry him into office had never before been his problem; Severne and his following had borne that task. Now Severne was abandoning him, was openly disparaging him.

"Give me your gun and let's go," he repeated. In an effort to regain lost stature he took his foot off the bottom stair and stood straight. But it was no good. The ridiculous swallow-tail coat helped to defeat the effect. "Dammit!" he muttered, reaching under it.

"Bring that hand out clean!" Madigan warned.

At the parlor door Arabella gazed wide-eyed up at him, oblivious of Severne's curt motion to her to go back into the parlor. Frowning, Severne pushed toward her, his benevolent chivalry discarded, jostling women as well as men, intent upon putting force into his command to her. Shade and Redlinger watched him, faintly critical, as they might have watched a man whose misbehaving horse made a nuisance of itself. Two more men joined them. The four shuttled glances, and at Shade's nod they separated.

"A lot of you are cleaned out! And burned out!" Madigan talked fast. He had to. The women were leaving, shepherded by Dr. Osborne. As they filtered out to safety, the faces of the men remaining behind portrayed a hardening temper.

"I came here from the Romedy camp. I heard three big herds being run off! I saw fires!" He also had to pick his words, not tip his hand too soon. First give them the picture, then the final fact that created it.

"The Romedy camp is where those herds are bound! That's where we're all going!" Severne had stopped by Arabella, his thick fingers gripping her shoulder. "We'll wipe it out, once and for all!"

His words stirred a storm of voices. Departing women lingered to look back. Men gestured at them to go on, hurry, get out of the hall. Severne couldn't let it lie at that, though. A worship of property, and the conviction that his listeners shared his devotion, led him on to bellow, "Don't worry, friends, we'll get your cows back! And the Romedys' horses will go a long way to pay for damage done! We'll —

"That many cattle couldn't be rafted over

215

the Pecos in a week!" Madigan broke in. "You won't find 'em anywhere near the Romedy camp — it's the worst crossing in miles. Their route's way farther northward, maybe to above Fort Stockton. Then over the Pecos and on to the New Mexico line. Like your calves!"

He had them listening and he rushed on. "A few calves don't leave much trail to follow, if they're kept scattered out. And you've all been fed the idea right along that the Romedys rafted 'em over at their camp. But Calhoun never found any actual proof of it."

"No, I didn't," Calhoun sourly admitted. It stood against his record. " 'Cept one time we caught a feller that was helping 'em run off a bunch of calves."

"And you didn't look anywhere else very hard, you've been so sure you're right. Well, this time it's more than a few calves. It's a clean sweep! You weren't meant to find it out till you all dragged home tomorrow from this party. Then you'd mill around in a sweat before finally charging off to the Romedy camp, where they'd put up a fight. Those cattle have got to leave a trail somewhere, but you'd all be too bonehead busy to look for it till too late! The thieves figure on getting all the start they need. That's why they picked tonight."

Arabella uttered a small cry, taking a step forward from the parlor door, her wide eyes incredulous. Severne shoved her urgently into the parlor, mussing her bridal veil, and turned his back on her to send Shade a straight look.

"My wedding night!" he growled. "They used my wedding to rob my friends!"

"They did," Madigan agreed, "according to plan." The last of the women had left the hall. "This raid was laid out for 'em like an organized roundup. They know what they're doing. About fourteen riders are in on it, I'd say."

Calhoun, one eye half shut in querying doubt, squinted up at him. "You talking about the Romedy men? Fourteen?"

"Take a look round you." Madigan spoke for the benefit of the crowd, not personally to Calhoun, whose belated spark of wisdom was brightening of its own accord. "Severne's wedding party has brought nearly everybody to town for the night — and yet some are missing who you'd most expect to be here. They're not missed in all the goings-on, folks circulating around town. There's Shade, and there's Redlinger, but they're official. They're law officers. They'd be missed. Only two other H 7 men here to represent the crew. Rondle and Volkman."

"You know their names. That's queer, you a stranger to these parts." Calhoun looked about him. He asked loudly, "Any more H 7 men here?" Receiving no response, he said, "Seems you're right."

"That makes about fourteen men — H 7 men — not accounted for, Sheriff!"

"And where" — Calhoun hesitated, torn between discretion and duty — "where are they?"

"Ask Severne!"

Men eyed Severne questioningly, thrown off-tack by the abrupt tangent and its significance. He reared up his head, roaring, "What the hell's this, Calhoun? My men are all here in town!"

"They're not," Madigan said to Calhoun. "You can guess where they are and what they're doing, and what they've done!" He had a fleeting stab of remorse at putting Calhoun on the spot, an aging man, none too bright, Severne's discarded tool. "Watch out for yourself, Sheriff, you're a dead duck if you side with me! Get out of it!"

"You go to hell!" muttered Calhoun. He plucked a pistol out from under his swallow-tail coat, a cap-and-ball .35 five-shot, the barrel sawed off to a snubby inch; a gun fashioned for unobtrusive wear and for use at close quarters. But indecision assailed him when he looked at Severne's face. Shaking the pistol like a school teacher's pointer, he announced, "I'm forming a posse to go after those cattle thieves, whoever they are!"

Behind Severne, from the parlor, Arabella called out, "Jim! Jim Madigan!"

Severne spun around. "What? What's that you say?"

"Jim!" she repeated distinctly. A kind of laughter, close to hysteria, heightened her voice to shrillness. "Jim Madigan!"

"You're crazy! Him?" Severne swung back, scowling his embarrassment at her untimely outburst. His stare at Madigan grew fixed, piercing. "Him? No, he's just a — he's —"

Then the shocked pause. The glare of recognition. The wild rage.

"Shade, you sonofabitch, you swore he was killed!"

"He was! He was!" Shade refused to believe it: a man risen from the dead. "He ain't Madigan! Can't be!" He exploded an oath. "Begod, he is! I know him now!"

"Get him, damn you!"

XVIII

Redlinger, having his gun already out, only had to tip it up and pull trigger. In his haste he nicked the edge of the big bronze urn and spun it, clanging like a bell, off its resting place on top of the newel post. For a moment the air was full of peacock feathers. His next bullet went yards wide, Madigan slinging a shot that twisted him on his legs.

Rondle and Volkman, acting as a two-man team, opened fire and advanced together. They were both young men, hot to build a record and rise in Severne's book, competing with Shade for top honors. Shade, unruffled by their eager blazing and the uproar, batted an iridescent-eyed tailfeather away from his face and sought to score a hit from where he stood.

Calhoun backed off in dismay from the bottom of the stairs, bumping into Volkman, who was coming up behind him and using him as a convenient shield. Volkman swore at him, while Rondle eeled on past to earn lone credit. Scrambling backward up the stairs, Madigan spent a shell on Rondle.

Shade fired. He called coolly to Severne, "I hit him!"

"He's still on his feet!"

"Won't be for long!"

In a crossfire predicament, Calhoun took the course of combining discretion with duty. "Get outside, you men!" he shouted. "I'm forming a posse!" He would not take a stand against Severne without complete evidence, and whatever happened to Madigan was beyond his control.

Men were swarming at all possible exits, prodding by anxiety for their cattle as well as the flare-up of gunfire in the hall. Calhoun's pronouncement served no hastening purpose, but it placed an official stamp on the exodus and justified his active part in it.

Crouched, Madigan dragged himself farther up the stairs. The edge of the staircase hid Shade from him, and in the pandemonium below it became difficult to keep track of Volkman. Rondle was out of the fight. Without his partner, Volkman gained the caution to dodge into the thinning crowd and shoot while on the move.

Severne rapped, "Quit fooling and get him!"

As the hall rapidly cleared, noise outside increased, horses and wheeled rigs clattering off up the street. Calhoun wasn't getting time for any formal swearing-in of possemen, unless he did it at a gallop.

Bereft of the covering crowd, Volkman stood and took aim, calling out, "Shade — now!"

With his elbow braced on the edge of a stair, Madigan fired at him. His elbow slipped. He missed. Volkman flinched, steadied his arm, and called once more for Shade.

"Go to it, kid!" Shade answered. "He can't have more'n two shells left in his gun! Make him shoot 'em off!"

Unnerved by the knowledge that Shade was using him to draw Madigan's fire, Volkman darted low behind the couch on which the body of old Sam Coble lay and lined his sights over it. On the floor, Rondle raised a white face; and groped for his fallen gun.

Madigan fired at Volkman before shifting to menace Rondle with his last shell. Shade then made his move, easing in close alongside the staircase. Madigan got a sudden glimpse of his face stretched upward for a sight of him. He brought his gun over to poke through the bannister rails and drive Shade back by its threat, but Shade had come too near for him to give way. Both fired at the same instant.

A crash in his head jerked a convulsive protest from Madigan's muscles. Rolling down the stairs, sure that half his head was torn off, he instinctively tried to protect it with his arms. His brief roll ended. He lay on the bottom stairs and listened to Shade say, "I'll finish him!"

He could see Shade in a swimming haze, pressing a hand to his neck to stem blood from a bullet wound. Then Severne, moving fast to the foot of the stairs and bulking in front of Shade.

Severne said, "No, he's mine!" He held a gun cocked in his hand. "Twice you botched it! Twice!" he berated Shade, with the bitterness of a man whose hired help had unforgivably failed his trust. "You and Redlinger!"

"I'd have got him!" Shade argued, holding his neck.

"After he emptied his gun! After he set half the county on the trail of those cattle!"

"That wasn't any o' my doing!"

"Shut up! Be hell to pay if they catch up with the crew!" Severne stooped forward. "Look at me, Madigan! Look me in the eyes while I shoot you! I'll leave no damn ghost to come back this time!"

Arabella screamed. Madigan supposed she had come out of the parlor; he couldn't see her. Severne raised his head. "Get back in there!" he ordered. Then suddenly his face changed. He and Shade spun around, and through the space between them Madigan saw four men standing inside the front door: Shep Romedy and his two eldest sons, Blair and Jared; and Silent Lionel. They carried rifles. They let Severne and Shade make the first lethal move to shoot at sight of them.

Silent Lionel's rifle flashed. Three more swift reports, and each of the four men snapped a fresh cartridge into the breech. Severne continued raising his gun, raising it high, until he toppled backward and fell beside Shade. It was over in seconds. Arabella screamed again.

Silent Lionel, his gaze as remote as ever, looked at Rondle on the floor. Rondle lowered his face and played dead. Shep spoke to Madigan.

"When we do get involved in somebody's affairs, we go all the way. If you're finished here, we'll take you home."

Madigan tried to speak. A cold sickness numbed him. Their faces were fading.

Arabella appeared, a white-gowned wraith shimmering through thickening darkness. The Romedy men moved aside for her to go to Henry Severne, her dead husband. But it was over Madigan that she bent, crying, "Jim! You're hurt — you're hurt bad!"

She hitched up her satin skirt and knelt by him. "You came back to me! Doctor — !"

The last he heard was Shep saying with wintry regret, "I guess you're not finished here. S'long, Jim Madigan. . . ."

He lay listening to Dr. Osborne telling him that Sheriff Calhoun's informal posse had trailed the cattle and brought them back; that there had been no fight because the H 7 riders had bolted off when they'd spied the pursuing mob.

"It appears that Severne was an utter scoundrel," the doctor said. "I would have lost the money I'd invested in heavy mortgages on those cattle. Practically every dollar I own. Think of it! Think of the duplicity of that man!"

You think of it, Madigan wanted to say. *I'm gathering my thoughts on something else. But I'm lying here in a bed in your house, so I owe you some politeness.*

"He wanted the springs, you see," Dr. Osborne explained from his superior and enlightened wisdom. "To get them he would have ruined these smaller ranchers. I can't see why they were so stupid, so blind! Of course, they know now that they, er, misjudged you — as far as stealing their calves is concerned, that is. I'm sure the sheriff will not press other charges, if you talk to

225

him in a proper spirit. People are on your side."

"My side hurts," Madigan said. "Up near my left arm. And my head." He touched his bandaged head. "Not as much as I'd expect, though. Just aching."

"I've kept you under drugs. You were restless much of the time." Dr. Osborne picked up a medicine phial from the bedside table and slipped it into his coat pocket. "You'll feel some discomfort for a while, but you're on the mend. All you need is rest. You have a remarkably strong constitution. I daresay it's due to your outdoor life. Fresh air, plain food, that sort of thing." He had no idea of how fresh the air could be in a winter camp up north, how plain the food for a penniless drifter.

"I've got to get dressed." Madigan struggled out of the bed. "Where's my clothes?"

"No, no that won't do at all!" The doctor pushed him back to the bed. "We want you to get well."

"I'm well enough." Madigan steadied his shaking legs. "My clothes!"

Dr. Osborne took the medicine phial from his pocket. "I think," he said, "I'd better give you something to sleep."

"No more dope!"

"Madigan, I insist that you go back to bed! Listen, I have a message for you. It will ease your mind."

"From the Romedys? From Dare?"

"Er, no. From Arabella. The exposure of Henry Severne's rascality," the doctor expounded, "has gone far to, er, remove her grief — eliminate it, I might say — over his death. And, after all, he *was* so much older. She has moved out to the Severne ranch. As his widow," he mentioned pointedly, "she is the primary claimant to his whole estate. I advised her to take immediate possession."

He paused expectantly. Locating his clothes — they were hung in an open closet — Madigan turned, stumbled, and nearly fell on him.

Receiving no better cooperation, the doctor came right out with it. "Arabella wishes you to call on her when you are able."

"Where'd they put my horse?"

"Hm? It's at the livery stable, I believe. But really, there's no need to hurry. This is absurd!" The doctor indulgently shook his head. These Westerners. So unthinking. Uncivilized. "For one thing, you must wear better clothes than those. You must shave, cut your hair, look presentable to her. Don't worry, she'll wait for you."

"Right," Madigan said. "She'll wait."

■ ■ ■ ■

The Romedys were gone from their campsite on the Pecos. Long gone. Only the big
raft remained. From up on the high bluffs
Madigan saw it lying on the far bank. The
log raft had served first to float their wagons
over to the bluffs-hemmed stronghold, and
at last to float them out again. Anybody who
wanted to could use the raft now.

He cursed the quieting drugs and pain
killers, realizing that the doctor had kept
him in a stupor for days and nights — how
many, he didn't know and hadn't thought
to ask.

"Dare!" he whispered. "Dare!"

Dare, not hearing any word from him to
sustain her faith, must have finally broken
down and agreed to leave, believing he was
finished with her.

But surely a voice inside her cried that she
was his woman, that he would come after
her wherever she went. Didn't the Romedy
understand that they were his people?

Calling to mind Jaffah's description of
their proposed route, he scouted downriver
for miles until tracks at a shallow ford
showed him definitely that the wagons had
crossed back over to the west bank, and he

set out on the long slant to the Big Bend and on down.

By the time he skirted under the Santiago Mountains he was holding onto the saddle horn. A short rest, and he pushed on, alternately walking and loping. Drifting sand covered the wagon tracks in places, but the black horse never strayed far off it, knowing by smell or by some other sense that its mates had passed this way.

That night he lay listening to the fluttering wail of a whippoorwill and the imbecilic snicker of a night bird that he didn't recognize. At Grapevine Spring the keeper of the one store had told him he looked bad, very bad. Madigan believed him; he knew he was on the verge of collapse.

The Grapevine Spring storekeeper was a Mexican, and finding that Madigan had taken the trouble to pick up some kitchen-Spanish, he had offered to show him a hideout where the law wouldn't find him.

"Mil gracious," Madigan had said, "but I am chasing a woman. My woman."

"Ah!" The storekeeper had smiled understandingly, looking at his bandaged head. "You fought for her, and you will fight again, yes? It is good to be young, to be virile." He had given Madigan some jerky and cold tortillas, and an old canteen.

A rest of more than an hour or two couldn't be afforded. It stiffened him so he could hardly climb back on the saddle. He got up and rode on, and in the dawn he passed between Paint Gap Hills to where the land spread out barren and bone dry. He had hunted for wild cattle down here.

By noon the black suffered from thirst and showed signs of giving out, but it was hours more before they reached Tornillo Springs, where Madigan watered the horse and filled his canteen. The horse needed rest and so did he. He gave barely an hour to it, and rode up a long rise, topping out to where he could see Alsate Bluff dead ahead, a red profile against the blue-hazed Chisos Mountains much further on. At sundown he made dry camp under Alsate Bluff until moonlight. He wasn't too far behind the Romedy wagons now, he judged. The tracks of them were clean. Maybe tomorrow. . . .

The next day he was talking aloud, saying over and over the words he would say when he caught up with Dare. Sometimes he fancied he was saying them to her; then his senses would come jolting back to reality.

He passed Moss Wells and Water Barrels — no water there anymore — and the ancient ghost-prison of San Vicente where doomed convicts had once taken a one-way tramp to work themselves to death in secret goldmines for a grasping governor.

"Louse!" he muttered, remembering the legend.

Caballo Muerto, Mount Emory, Boot Canyon — the drooping black went lame in Boot Canyon. He had to trudge alongside, his arm over its neck to save himself from falling. Forty-Mile Post and Palma Canyon, utterly silent, not a bird to be seen. The endless, hideous plodding brought him to Dagger Flats.

The giant yuccas of Dagger Flats reared their heavy cream-white blossoms in huge clusters, astonishingly high; they resembled colossal lilies flowering over a mammoth graveyard. Madigan was spent, a skeleton tottering in wrecked boots, his feet blistered and bloody. He peered at the sight before him: white-capped hussars on stiff legs thirty feet tall, with bundles of six-foot spurs at their heels. His hunts for wild cattle had never brought him this far south. No cow could hope for a living here.

He saw the big Romedy wagons marching steadily in line through the ranks of yuccas, and the band of black horses, dust hanging behind in a low-lying cloud. His limping horse nickered, letting him know that it wasn't a mirage, it was real.

He tried to send forward a hail. It came out as a croak.

"Oh, God!" he mumbled. "Make 'em stop and let me catch up. Dare, look back — it's me."

Because of the weight, he had hung his gun and belt on the saddle horn. He dragged the gun from its holster, and fell to his knees. It wasn't loaded. He got a shell from the belt, fumbled it into the cylinder, and squeezed the trigger. The horse hopped at the discharge.

Slowly, the canvas-topped wagons settled to a standstill. One of them — he knew the one — swung out of line and careened in a half-circle, its driver lashing the team. It straightened out and rocked toward him, side-swiping yuccas, trailing billows of dust.

He kept his eyes on the driver. *Here comes my home,* he thought with bottomless gladness. *My woman, my heart, my life. My querencia.*

We hope you have enjoyed this Large Print book. Other Thorndike, Wheeler, and Chivers Press Large Print books are available at your library or directly from the publishers.

For information about current and upcoming titles, please call or write, without obligation, to:

Publisher
Thorndike Press
295 Kennedy Memorial Drive
Waterville, ME 04901
Tel. (800) 223-1244

or visit our Web site at:

www.gale.com/thorndike
www.gale.com/wheeler

OR

Chivers Large Print
published by BBC Audiobooks Ltd
St James House, The Square
Lower Bristol Road
Bath BA2 3SB
England
Tel. +44(0) 800 136919
email: bbcaudiobooks@bbc.co.uk
www.bbcaudiobooks.co.uk

All our Large Print titles are designed for easy reading, and all our books are made to last.